The Widower

Written by J. W. Carter

Edited by Michelle Holt

DEDICATION

This book is dedicated to my family and friends that
have given me a lifetime of stories and characters I look
forward to sharing.

CONTENTS

ACKNOWLEDGMENTS

It's not easy to create a character who loses his wife especially when you're still happily married. I truly love and appreciate her understanding that I had a story to tell. I only hope through 'killing a wife in print,' I can provide a better life for my own in reality. This book is dedicated to the woman who supports me through everything and loves me even when I do things that would cause most women to walk out the door.

CHAPTER 1
THE CALL

"Well hello Molly, this is Drew." I sat there for a second and then whispered; "Oh-My-God." My voice changed from surprised to excited. "Oh Drew, how are you? Are things alright? How are the kids?" I was talking so fast I didn't know if he could understand the multiple syllables all squished into one. But he stopped me before I could continue my rambling. "Everybody's doing well, Moll. It's been a while since we talked. How are things at the TV station?" "Everything is the same as usual, bullshit combined with the absurd. It's so good to hear from you. I've been meaning to call and check in, but I didn't want to wake the baby or disturb you at work…" I couldn't help but sound guilty. But he took over the conversation before I could make a bigger fool of myself. "Don't worry about it. I've got keys on my phone, I should have called sooner."

"Oh, Drew I hate to say this, but we just pulled in for an interview and I've gotta go get this guy on camera. Can I call you back? I really want to hear about Mobile and Greer, Eli and little Walker…" He cut me off again. "Sure, but I have a quick question. What are you doing in a couple weeks?" He sounded scared, so confused I replied, "I don't know. Are you coming into town?" In his quick interrupt fashion Drew continued his inquiry. "Would you want to come down to Mobile?" Huh, is the only thing that came to mind. So I sat there for what seemed an eternity and then reluctantly spoke; "Drew, I'd love to come down but getting a ticket last minute, and a vacation request, I'm not sure I could swing that..." He didn't let me finish. "Don't worry about the plane ticket, I'll get that. And we can work out the rest of the details later. Why don't you ask the boss lady if you can have a three day weekend at the end of the month? I'll arrange everything else." Again I was very confused and not sure what to say. "Ok, I'll call you tonight or tomorrow," I said with a great deal of apprehension. "I look forward to it. Just let me know what days are best for you and we'll go from there? It was great to hear your voice; talk soon." Still in a little bit of shock I replied, "great- talk soon."

"Was that Drew Chandler?" My photographer, Bill, turned to me and asked. "Yeah." And without even looking up from my phone I said, "He wants me to come down to Mobile. Is that kind of weird?"

Bill replied, "I don't think it's weird. You guys were friends before his wife died." I sat there and looked at Bill behind the wheel of the Ford Escape dashboard. "Yeah, but he wants to pay for my flight and I don't know what else. I don't know, maybe I'm just a little shocked by the whole thing. After all, I haven't spoken to him since the funeral even though I promised to keep in touch. I kind of feel like a big selfish bitch right now." Bill laughed, "You are a selfish bitch. But obviously he wants to see you or he wouldn't have called and invited you to visit. Wow! He used to be like Mr. sarcastic, happy, fun loving. But the look on his face at the funeral with those kids in his arms, geez, I don't know. I'm more surprised to hear that he's still alive than the fact he called you."

I stared at Bill and had a flashback of the memorial service when Drew stood and spoke before the crowd; "Don't worry about me, and please spare me your prayers. I lost my better half, but I still have memories. But these kids lost everything. So when you get on your knees and think about this family, I ask for your blessings to be with these little ones. Because they will never know just how unbelievable their mother was." He loved

her so much and now he wanted me to come hang
out.

The rest of the day I couldn't stop thinking
about him. I did my interviews, wrote my story, all
the while reliving the times Drew had made fun of
me or listened to me when I bitched. I kind of
missed it. He wasn't the kind of person you ever
forgot. He had a sick child but was always playful
and unserious. He was passionate about what he
did; news in general, but it didn't consume him like
other journalists. He used to joke that I was his
"work wife" since we shared an anchor desk. I
really did want to see him. But what would this
visit be? I mean after all, he's single now. Is it a
date? Is he dating? Is it too early to date? I mean
his wife died less than a year ago. Am I his
rebound? Or is it merely a friendship thing? But
why would you pay a few hundred dollars for a
friendly visit? I was so confused and it was near
show time. Once again I had broken a promise to
him, I didn't ask for the time off or call him back.

CHAPTER 2
THE DECISION

After a sleepless night, thinking about him and how nice it would be to get out of Iowa, I called my boss to ask for the time off. "Hey June, it's Molly." June in her usual I'm doing twenty other things so make it quick tone said, "What's up?" "Can I take a day at the end of the month? I'll take off like a Wednesday to go along with my Monday, Tuesday days off." "What day specifically do you want?" June asked in her, this could have been done in an email. "How's the 29th of June?" "Ok, just fill out the paperwork, but I've got it in the calendar. Are you going home?" June asked. When she did, I almost didn't know what to say. It wasn't like I was doing anything wrong, was I? So I just let it slip out. "I'm going down to Mobile to see Drew and his family." June made an instant aghast. "Oh My God! How is he? I've emailed and called him a few times but he never gets back to me. I was so scared something might happen to him. Are the kids doing alright? Oh that little Walker is one of the most beautiful creatures I've ever seen. How did he sound when you talked to him? Is Greer still having seizures? Is he still a bit of a recluse? I heard he's still in mourning. Oh God, I wish I could just talk to him." June's barrage of questions just kept going and I stopped listening. He was so destroyed the last time any of us talked to him, now he wants me to be his shoulder to cry on. Dammit, what was I doing? Now everybody in the TV station was going to harass me with questions about him. I don't know what to say. I don't what all 'this' means. He has a full plate of stuff going on. Why would he want to entertain me? I'll just call him, tell him I can't get the days off and prevent this reunion from taking place. But, I really do want to see him. He was my friend, I mean, he is my friend. I guess the least I can do is go down and cry with him for a few days.

Before I went into work I called him. I didn't have his number in my phone so I had to go through my call log. The 251 area code made it easy to find. So after pushing the call button on my phone, one ring, and a woman answered the phone; "Good morning, Chandler & Associates. Can I help you?" This must be his work number. His Dad owned a company in Mobile and that must be where he's working now. "Yes, can I speak with Drew Chandler please?" She quickly rebuked, "I'm sorry he's unavailable right now. Is there anything I can help you with?" Good, he's busy. "No, I'll just call…" "Oh, Ms. Burke he was expecting your call. Can I transfer you to his cell phone?" Ok, he told the receptionist to be expecting me, that's weird. "Sure, I guess that'll be alright. Am I going to catch him at a bad time though?" She laughed, "No, it may be hard to hear him. But I'm sure he can step away from his chocolate milk and Salisbury steak. He has lunch with one of his kids nearly every day. Today he's with Greer. Let me connect you. I'm so glad you called." That makes no sense. 'I'm so glad you called. He's expecting your call.' What is he telling people at work? Yeah, I'm pretty sure I'll just tell him I can't get away and this is not happening. Whatever 'this' is?

"This is Drew." It sounded like he was at a concert. "Hey, it's me, Molly." Drew started talking loud and fast; "Oh hey sweetheart, my apologies I'm at an incredibly crowded…hah, I'm having lunch with my daughter." I think he was trying to make what he was doing sound more important. His insecurities were occasionally charming. However, I had made up my mind that I was going to put my foot down and tell him that he 'is' my friend but I'm just too busy. But I didn't. "How's the 27th thru the 29th? " He sounded like he was going to jump through the phone. OUTSTANDING! I'll have the flight arrangements in your inbox within fifteen minutes. Do you have a preference on airports? Seats? Would you like to stay with me? Or would you like a hotel? Do you want to golf? Go to the beach? Swim? Go to a casino? Oh wait, we'll talk about that later. Let me get your flight. I'll get you an early morning flight on the 27th and a late flight on the 29th. Does that work? Do you still have the same email?" Wow, he didn't breathe during that entire rambling. I was freaked out. "Yeah, same email. Everything sounds great to me but we can just play it by ear on what we do, and when? Is that alright?" He took a big breath in, "yeah, I'm really excited you're coming. I'll have your flight information to you within the hour. Just give me a call or text if you have things you want to do or if you need help with luggage, a ride to the airport, or whatever. Alright?" What could I say? "Ok, we'll talk soon."

One minute later, my phone beeped to tell me I had an email. In my inbox was one ticket with a layover in Atlanta from Cedar Rapids to Mobile. It was 458 dollars and non-refundable. I guess I was committed and all I had done was say 'yes.'

It was fifteen days and counting and I had no idea what I was preparing for. There were some people at work who had heard that I had talked to him and asked how he and his family were doing? Early on, nobody seemed to realize that I was going to see him, nor did I volunteer the information. The first person to find out my intentions, other than my boss-who remarkably kept the rendezvous quiet, was my Mom. "When you get here for your sister's birthday, I need you to stay a day longer and help me watch Chris. Kristen and Robert are going away for a couple of days. It's the first time they've had a vacation since Chris was born." My sister's birthday. How could I forget my visit to Mobile was smack dab in the middle of the party my Mom was planning for her? It was her 30th.

"Mom, I'm sorry I won't be able to help. I forgot to mention I'm going out of town that week." There were a few seconds of silence and I could feel my Mom was about to explode. "What do you mean you're going out of town? You're going to be home for your sister's birthday. I invited some of your friends from college. I've got your cousins coming in from Indianapolis. I don't understand how you could plan a trip when you know how important this was to your sister." Parents' yelling at kids always yields the same result, resentment and backlash. Even when parents are right. "I'm 27 years old I and don't need you approving my schedule. While it may have been a mistake to plan a trip that week it was something that suddenly came up and felt I needed to do. Anyways I'll see Kristen before her birthday. Maybe I'll join the party via Skype for a little while." Her tone suggested my logical solution wasn't good enough. "What could you possibly have planned 'LAST MINUTE,' that is more important that your sister's 30th?" Each word was like a dagger cutting into me. "A friend of mine lost his wife a year ago and he asked that I come south and spend time with him. I know he's had it rough and he offered to pay my way down. So I agreed to go." Another pregnant pause, but this time I knew she was furious. "So you're going SOUTH, to hang out with a widower, who's paying for you to visit? I have no idea what to say. Are you going down for a romantic visit? Are you just friends? Why is he paying your way?" My Mom's question recap was the most concise version of an illogical paradox playing in my head daily. Why was I going? What was I doing? "Mom it's complicated."

CHAPTER 3
MY GUY

A couple days before I was set to leave, a guy that I off and on dated/hooked up with, sent me a text. He wanted to "get a drink tonight and talk." This typical correspondence meant he wanted to come over or have me over for a couple hours. It wasn't anything serious, just sex. He was fun and great in bed. Drew, and I think one other person, ever openly suggested that Mike and I had a thing. After all, Mike is fifty one. I'm twenty seven. I know it seems kind of gross but he has a great body, tone, tan. He didn't look his age and didn't act it either. Five to six nights a week, he drank with 'twenty something' year old producers and reporters. Each night was full of Yeager shots and imported beer on tap. He was kind of the coolest guy in school, and I was sleeping with him.

The problem was he had a long distance girlfriend who he talked about marrying someday. Our relationship, if that's what you want to call it, was only temporary. But we both knew it and there was an understanding. However I didn't date, I just hooked up with him or an occasional guy at a party.

So I figured a little sex might take the edge off this upcoming trip.

Seated at a tavern, we didn't often go to, Mike started in. "So you're going to see Drew on Monday?" Here we were at a bar, almost like a date, and my guy on the side, WHO HAD A GIRLFRIEND, was all of a sudden inquisitive about my visit to see a friend. "Yeah, he called me a couple weeks ago and said he wanted to hang out. I feel so bad for just ignoring him after his wife died." Before I could continue, Mike interrupted. "That's the way this business works. We work with hundreds of different people who come and go, that's it. Shit, I've been doing this for nearly three decades, people leave. New jobs, family situations, new whatever's-people just go." Mike wasn't jealous but he was acting really weird. Plus, I hated when he brought up how long he'd been a news anchor, since it was longer than I had been alive. "Mike, I know how the migration of TV people works. It's just Drew was a co-worker and a friend. He's been through a lot and I just want to check-up on him. It's no big deal. Why are you so, whatever right now?" Mike did his usual shift in his chair, eyes glancing to both sides as if to make sure something hadn't fallen off the table beside us. "I just think it's a bad situation for you get into. He's got three kids. He's probably living off Daddy's money right now, and he's most definitely not stable. I mean Molly c'mon, he just called you out of the blue and said let me fly you down. Don't you find that odd? Don't you think you should at least question his motives? You're such a smart girl, but sometimes you're so naïve."

He just called me a kid and a moron all in the same speech. Now I was pissed. "Mike, I've got to go home, I've got a couple stories to work on in the morning before work. I'll talk to you later." Mike's face filled with surprise. "What? I thought we'd go back to my place and have a drink. (Wink, wink) Why are you leaving so soon? C'mon, I'm sorry. I won't meddle, I'm just concerned about you and I care about you. I'm sorry, I won't do that anymore. Please, let's get another round." In hind sight, this decision shouldn't have been so difficult. I should have just grabbed my purse and hit the door. But Mike was fun and he'd still be my friend when I got back home. So, I sat down and had another round.

CHAPTER 4
SECOND THOUGHTS

The weekend before I left, the newscasts were incredibly difficult to read. To start, when I came out for the first show of the night, my co-anchor was incredibly sarcastic and perverted. This was weird for a guy who was typically so self- absorbed. It was completely out of character. Our conversations' usually consisted of his ties, his suit color clashing with mine, or some script he loathed reading. But instead he was cutting up like Drew did before every show. I kept seeing Drew in everything he said. The flashbacks went on even when the show was in progress.

Needless to say, I stumbled my way through an hour and half of news. Even the producer asked me if I was sick after the second show on Saturday. "You're just not yourself, Moll. What's up? Are you feeling ok? Cameron showed you up all night. What's going on?" I didn't want to break down my apprehensions or even let Ryan, the producer, into my plans next week. "I don't know Ryan; I've just got a lot on my mind. Plus, my agent can't seem to get me any interviews worth taking and I've got six months left on my contract. I'm just starting to get worried that's all. I really don't want to re-sign here and June's pressuring me."

The greatest diversion tactic in TV news, talk about problems you're having with your agent or your inability to make the leap to your next station. "Moll, I wouldn't worry about it, you're great! Your agent will find you something soon. Just make sure today's shows don't hit your reel." He walked away chuckling. I sat there red faced and my stomach, which was a chronic problem, began to churn. If this was the right thing to do I wouldn't be pissing everybody off; my producer, my mom, my bootie call....What was I doing?

On Sunday more of the same and I was in even more abdominal pain. I floated through the day aggravating myself with thoughts that it wasn't too late to cancel. Just before I was about to go to dinner my cell rang, it was Drew. Up to this point, we really hadn't talked. We just sent a text here and there with some ideas for the week. "Hey, shouldn't you be out to eat or putting those damn curlers in your hair?" It had been a year since anybody ragged me for the curlers I used to add body to my hair on TV. "Gotta look good for the great people of Eastern Iowa." That was easy. "Ah, shit you could go out there in T-shirt and jeans and blow them away. It's not your hair they're staring at!" Is that flirting? If it is, he's been flirting with me way before his wife died. "You're too sweet. Well my bag is packed and I'm heading to the airport at 7:30." Just hearing his voice was starting to remove the weight in my chest and stomach. I couldn't tell what he was feeling. He just seemed giddy, which was the guy I remembered. "Good to hear. I'll come get you at 1:15 and we'll go get lunch. While we eat we'll discuss and finalize an itinerary. Like I said last week, if we play golf, I'll rent you some clubs. Don't try and drag them to the airport. Just pack light and we'll have a great time." I wanted to question him about the week. If this was a social visit, or a friend thing, or what? But I didn't because he seemed so happy. Honestly, I was pretty anxious too. But I wasn't sure what I was anxious for. "Just call me when you get to the airport in Cedar Rapids to let me you know you're ok." That was a pretty easy request. "I will. Have a good night and I'll see you tomorrow."

While I told Drew I had finished packing, I sort of hadn't. In fact, I hadn't packed a thing. For guys it's easy; a pair of jeans, a few button up shirts, a couple pairs of shorts if it's warm, maybe a pair of khaki's. For girls, it's different. If I'm going on a date, I might wear a skirt or a more revealing shirt. The more I like the guy the more I'm willing to show. If I'm hanging out with the girls I might just wear a pair of jeans, a tank top or t-shirt. But I had no idea what to pack. A sun dress would be wonderful in the south Alabama heat. But would that be interpreted as an invitation? Do I pack comfy panties or do I pack panties I might want somebody to see? And I couldn't pack my whole wardrobe because that would mean I was thinking about this week way too much. Also, and just as importantly, grooming. I would certainly shave my legs since I'd definitely be wearing shorts or a dress. I'd need to address my bikini line for swimming. BUT! Was this a situation I needed to prepare myself for a potential intimate showcasing? I sat there and looked in the mirror for what seemed an eternity and aired on the side of caution.

At 2am I finally laid in bed and pulled the sheets and comforter up to my chin. I lived in a one bedroom apartment that was cute and new. It wasn't big, but it was comfortable. My bedroom was completely dark other than the light on the oven which I could see from my bed. In four hours I was waking up and heading south. Going to see a guy who was here one day bragging about his wife, the money maker, and his new child. Then one day it all changed. I remember sitting at my desk, reading a Facebook message, when Eric-the assignment editor, yelled for everybody's attention. "Less than an hour ago, Drew's wife Lori, died. According to the post-natal nurse, they couldn't stop the bleeding after their baby boy was born. We'll be sending flowers, and getting a card for all of you to sign. The nurse said he does not want any visitors." In 2010, a woman dying in the midst of childbirth still sends chills down my back. Thank God they saved the baby. But while Lori was someone who was often the brunt of his jokes, he still loved her very much. He bragged about her. I couldn't imagine being in a relationship with somebody who was so proud of you that he had to talk about what you had accomplished. After she died I called, and went to his house, but nothing. He didn't talk to anybody, except June, who he told he was resigning to move closer to family.

The last time I saw him was at the funeral. A handful of us from the TV station caravanned to Memphis to be there with him. After the service, he thanked us all for coming but said little else. I hugged him at the end and told him I'd be praying for him. But he seemed to be looking through me the whole time. He wore sunglasses at the funeral and never took them off. I saw tears rolling down the sides of his face but the glasses served their purpose. From the moment we got there until we drove away, he never put down his two older kids. He just held them close. God, that was the last time I saw him, crying over his wife's dead body. I never did pray like I said I would. So I got down on my knees, next to my bed, closed my eyes, and said, "God watch over me. God keep Drew strong. Bless his amazing children...Our Father who art in heaven..."

CHAPTER 5
D-DAY

"Wake up, put on a little make up…" I hate
clock radios but they do get your attention. It was
time. I grabbed a Mountain Dew because I hate
coffee and turned on the news for a second. As
soon as I sat down my phone beeped, it was a text.
"Good morning, I just wanted to make sure you
didn't miss your plane…I know you sleep with that
damn phone. LOL! See you soon." We knew each
other for about nine months and he did seem to
know a lot about me. It was weird and made me
feel special since he still remembered.

"Don't you have a newscast to do Ms. Burke?"
The guy at the security checkpoint tried to flirt with
me as I was putting my flip flops in the container.
The scrutiny my ¼ inch plastic shoes get at the
airport never disappoints. "No, I get some days off
too. I'm getting out of town for a bit; get a little sun
maybe a tan." I was trying to talk slow enough that
my sentences would carry me through the entire
security line. It almost worked. "I'm sorry ma'am
we've got to check your bag." Well shit, this guard
is about to delve into my bag I quite literally

vacuum packed to fit twelve outfits in for a fifty hour trip.

"So, where you heading?" The latex gloved woman asked. "I'm heading to Mobile to see a friend of mine." I used my let's save the small talk tone and get you done with my bag. "Mobile, huh? Beautiful down there, hot though." I nodded. "By the way, whatever happened to the guy you used to do the shows with? I thought you guys were cute together. He seemed nice." A smile came over my face. "That's actually who I'm going to see." She perked up with a surprised look on her face. "Are you guys an item? I always thought he was of 'another persuasion.'" My brow furled. "Another persuasion?" She quickly retorted. "Yeah, I thought he was gay. White teeth always real tan." I wanted to laugh out loud. But I didn't want to extend this conversation nor explain the situation as I saw her zipping up my bag. "Well, at least he's fun to shop with…have a great day."

I walked away with the biggest grin, I wonder if I should tell Drew that Eastern Iowa people think I was the 'Grace' to his 'Will.' It's true, at times he could look almost too pretty on TV to be straight…ha, ha, ha.

As I walked to the gate, I started to think about him. In the past few weeks the only thing that came to mind was emotional images. Either him making me laugh or trying to empathize with him at the funeral. But when I take his 'gayness' into account, he was an attractive guy. I'd seen pictures of him taken before we met, which showed he was once in really good shape. He was tall and handsome, about 6 foot 3 inches, almost a foot taller than me. His hair was dark brown, nearly black, with grey mixed in on the sides. He had good facial features; nice eyes (usually blood shot), a natural smile, and big shoulders that made you feel safe when he was around. The last time I saw him, he wasn't necessarily fat but he wasn't trim either. He was carrying a bit of a beer gut. In fact, you could tell he was squeezing into pants that probably fit years ago. Not that he was slovenly dressed, but when his daughter was diagnosed with a seizure disorder he put his physical well- being to the side. He had been determined to spend every waking second with her at home or in the hospital. I could appreciate that. I imagine he wasn't much to look at without a shirt on. But he was a married Dad when I worked with him, who was he trying to impress?

Soon after getting on the plane, and despite being extremely anxious, I crashed. Typically I can't sleep on planes. But for the last few days I wasn't able to relax at night in anticipation of what was to come. So once we lifted off, I fell asleep. I dreamed, but not about him. Instead I was in Chicago, about to go on the air of my first show in the significantly bigger TV market. I had more money, ensuing fame, and I was on TV in front of all the people in high school who never imagined I'd be this amazing. It was the best feeling in the world. Giving people information, while everyone looked at me; it was glorious! This was my dream since I decided to be a TV journalist. Now I was six months away from the end of my contract and if my agent could pull it off, it would soon be a reality.

I had intentionally avoided any type of real relationship in order to prevent anything from getting in the way of my dream. It may seem selfish or callous, but it was what I wanted. I wanted to be the person people turned to when they needed to know something. I wanted to be the person people last saw before they went to sleep at night. I wanted my parents to see how good I was. I wanted my sister to brag to her friends about my success. I wanted it for me. I didn't want anything else, period.

As the pressure started to change in the cabin, and we were beginning our approach to Atlanta, I realized I forgot to call Drew. The question of his sexuality had really thrown my morning awry. Well, I'll just text him when I land in Atlanta.

Once we began to taxi on the runway, I turned my phone on and decided to shoot him a quick text. My phone immediately beeped with a message, two in fact. The first one was from Drew, go figure. "Hey, I know you probably got recognized in the airport, your ego went through the roof, and you forgot about me. Let me know when you get to Atlanta so I don't have to contact the Air Marshalls to frisk and fondle everybody in locating you....can't wait to see you-Drew."

The next message was from Mike. "Sorry about the other night, your affairs are your affairs. Look, I've been thinking we need to talk when you get back. I think we need to talk more about us." Wow! Leave it to Mike to drop a load on me when I least expect it. There's no "us." There are just two people who like to have a good time on occasion. Why was he saying this now? Why did he seem to care so much about Drew and me? Hell, Mike and I have had sex the night before he's flown to Texas to see his girlfriend. I don't make issues with "us." Why was he? Frankly, I didn't really want to talk or think about Mike for the next few days. I'm spending time with an old friend.

"In Atlanta….about to go grab a little breakfast, I should see you in a couple…Mol." That seemed like a simple enough message, right to the point. But not twenty seconds passed before my phone beeped again. "Don't eat too much I don't want it to affect your drinking. LOL, see you soon." That son of a bitch! I haven't seen or talked to him in a year and he's back calling me an alcoholic. He used to jest with me there wasn't a bar or party I could avoid. He was married with kids. He had a life at home. I lived in an empty apartment by myself. Why wouldn't I want to go hang out with friends after work? It's true I did go out just about every night, but I only had a couple drinks. Does that sound like the person at their first AA meeting before they stand and confess? "My name is Molly Burke and I am an Alcoholic."

For breakfast, I had a twelve dollar airport omelet with cheese. I didn't want bad breath or have to go to the bathroom on the plane. The nap had really helped. I was rejuvenated and a little excited. As they announced over the intercom it was time to start boarding the flight to Mobile, a sudden anxiety attack struck. This was truly my last opportunity to not go. Once I got on the plane I couldn't run through the airport in the hopes he wouldn't see me. But for some reason despite the attack, I wasn't as nervous as before. Sure this wasn't the ideal situation and I was pretty sure he wasn't the ideal guy, but it was going to be fun. Probably a little dramatic, but I was looking forward to it.

"Seat 6A," said the lady scanning my ticket. Alright here we go; in about an hour I'll be with a guy that I never really had a romantic feeling for in my life. For forty eight plus hours, I would be with him night and day. That's not that bad. If it's fun, it'll fly by. If it's not, it's just forty eight hours and I'll be back on a plane. Back to my life playing TV anchor-woman in the evening, workout-aholic in the morning and another type of 'aholic' into the night. Drew would have no trouble agreeing with my normal and easily sustainable life style. It was definitely all I needed.

CHAPTER 6
MOBILE IS HOT!

When the wheels touched down on the Mobile runway, it seemed like heat immediately entered the cabin. Damn I thought, I didn't realize how hot it is down here. I'm still in air conditioning but it seems like the humidity is already piercing me. For some reason, I decided to wear jeans and a tank top, but I could already tell this was too much clothing for Mobile heat. Sweat was running down my back and I began to stick to the pleather airplane seats. I'll walk off this plane, melt and he'll make fun of me all day long. Maybe I should change in the bathroom? My clothes are in my bag. No, I'll just wait and see what the air conditioning outside this suddenly cramped airplane is like. I wasn't worried about my encounter anymore. All I could think about was how hot it was and how I must immediately get off this sardine sweat box.

When we pulled up to the gate and opened the door, I realized the plane was so small that we were getting off on a rolling stair case. I was going to have to walk outside, to the airport, through this southern Hades. Shit! I have to change. I don't want anybody to see me when I get through my marathon journey in jeans, carrying a bag that weighs more than a ton of bricks. "Thanks for flying with us, hope you enjoy your stay in Mobile," said the flight attendant. "Is it always this hot?" I remarked. "Honey it's only June, give it a month and then you'll feel hot." Wow, I looked at the flight attendant in complete astonishment. It gets hotter than this.

Inside the airport, it was a comfortable 67 degrees with the air fluffing each stride through the terminal. There were palm trees in the distance you could see out the gate windows. It was beautiful when you didn't think you were going to melt. I looked for the airport exit, I didn't know if I should call or just go downstairs and look for him. I decided to take the escalator down and see if he was around. About halfway down the 120 foot escalator, I spotted him. Except it wasn't really the guy I thought I'd see. He was smiling big and waving to get my attention. If he hadn't spotted me first, I'm not sure I would have been able to pick him out, even with his gigantic smile. He looked different. First off, he was very tan and wearing glasses on his head. His hair looked wind-blown, but as if it intentionally was supposed to. Without a doubt, he'd lost a lot of weight and appeared extremely fit.

From about fifty feet away I could make out the muscle structure in his neck and shoulders. He was dressed casual but professional. He had a black blazer on that fit him perfectly, a white button up shirt made of some light cloth, and jeans that were stylish but not juvenile. His hair was lighter, obviously from time in the sun, and he was wearing flip flops. When I saw the shoes, I started to laugh, but he started talking first.

"Wow, you look amazing, let me get that bag." He spoke, hugged, and reached for my bag all at the same time. His arms and chest were hard, yet he was warm. "Oh my, somebody found a gym?" I didn't know what else to say. He quickly smiled, "Yeah, they have those down here. We work out after the Klan rallies." Never taking anything serious, that's Drew.

"How was your flight? You really do look amazing. I'm sorry it's so hot. The city has been trying to move further away from the equator." I found myself staring at his profile as we walked to the parking lot. "Everything was great. You didn't have to wait for me very long, did you? I noticed we were a few minutes late." Drew looked at his watch, a nice Movado with a burnt brown band. "Just a few minutes, it wasn't bad. I like the airport here. If it wasn't for the price of a flight, I'd fly out of here more often."

Just as we were getting close to his four door black wrangler with the top off, somebody started yelling, "Drew, Drew." Drew turned around and recognized the voice. "Holy shit, Dick Johnson! What are you up to man?" They quickly hugged each other as two old friends who hadn't seen each other in years. "Dude, I'm heading to New York for a few days. Did you just get back in town? Is this your wife?" Dick, as Drew called him, was an attractive thirtyish-looking fraternity boy. He was wearing a blue travel blazer, khakis, and a striped shirt. He also was tan with hair similar to Drew's new do.

"No this is a good friend of mine, Molly. Molly this is Richard Johnson, I prefer to call him Dick Johnson, based on the relative similarity to two, well, you know." I reached for Dick's hand as Drew finished his penis analogy. "Damn dude, I haven't seen you in probably five years. I heard you were on TV, popped out a few kids. Shit where are you now? Are you still on the tube?" Suddenly the heat of Mobile and the un-comfortableness of the ensuing conversation started to make me sweat.

"Well, I'm living in Mobile working with my Dad. I got out of TV and now I'm just looking for every way possible to make money and spend time with my kids." Drew said with a half-smile now. "Does your wife know you're hanging out with beautiful women like this Molly here?" Dick gave me a charming smile and a slight bow as if to show his desire to flatter me. Drew paused and you could tell he was searching for a way to answer the question. He looked down at his watch and then looked at Dick. "Hey man, I promised this beautiful lady I'd get here some un-oiled seafood and I'm already late on my promise. If you're living in Mobile, let's get together soon." Drew reached for his wallet, got out a business card and handed it to Dick. "Give me a shout when you get back from New York and we'll catch up." Dick looked a little surprised but he rolled with it. "Absolutely, I'm afraid I'm gonna miss my flight if I don't get my ass in there. It was great seeing you and I'll absolutely call you next week. Molly, it was a pleasure meeting you. Hopefully I'll get a chance to learn a little bit more about you soon."

I smiled, thankfully it was over. Not that Dick wasn't a southern charmer, but I wasn't ready for the "my wife is dead" speech and this is a girl who's come to stay with me for a couple days. As Drew turned towards the Jeep, Dick grabbed his leather duffle bag, his matching leather briefcase and was off.

"Let me throw your bag in the back. What did you pack a photographer in here? I'm surprised you didn't get scoliosis lugging this bad boy around the airport? Anything valuable in here?" I nodded my head no. And he threw my bag in the trunk. "Have you considered getting into the valet business with your genteel treatment of people's garment bags?" He smiled and brushed past me. He opened the door and bowed to welcome me into his off-road, military like, fully loaded jeep. "Let's get you some seafood?"

After he slammed the door on me and jogged to the driver's side, I looked in the back where his three car seats lined the second row. It looked like the Goldilocks story, with a large, medium and small seat. Once he was in the driver's seat and started the car and air, thank God; he started in on Dick. "Dick's an alright guy, we were in a fraternity together in High School." I looked at him surprised.

34

"Yeah, our high school was weird and had fraternities." He turned around to reverse out of the parking spot. "Anyway, he's one of those people I run into from time to time in Mobile. They always want to hang out when we meet and then I never hear from them. Its fine, I suppose. If I wanted to hang out, I'd probably call them." I just smiled at him as he popped his glasses back over his eyes.

The air in the jeep was blasting as the warm Mobile breeze was moving quickly over the roll bar. The airport was beautiful with the exit road lined with palm trees. I would never tell Drew, but the jeep was the perfect car to have in this environment. Even though, I worried with every turn he was going to flip me out. Tightly gripping the door handle, I searched for something to say. "So do you like living down here? It's not too hot for ya?" He smiled. "The first couple of months, the heat proved nearly unbearable. Especially after my time in Iowa. But it's grown on me. There's a big difference in being here as the seasons change as opposed to freezing your ass off up North and then trying to adjust to this climate." He was matter of fact, not as fun loving as when I first saw him. The conversation with Dick had him thinking; which is fine. If he wants to vent or hurt with me around, I'm prepared. It's more or less what I expected.

After we pulled out of the airport, Drew started to perk back up. "So what are you looking to eat? Do you want straight seafood? Seafood right out of the water? Cajun food? Tell me and I'll bring you there." It was good to see him smile again. "Whatever is fine with me, I'm just along for the ride. I'm fairly certain wherever we go it will be ten times better than what I'm used to." He started laughing. "Yeah, one thing I don't miss about Iowa are all the chain restaurants. Don't get me wrong, there are some good spots in Iowa but Mobile has some of the finest restaurants in the country. Let's go look out on the bay and eat a ton of food. Plus, its happy hour somewhere and I need to get you a drink." And just like that his sarcastic spirit returned. I really liked that Drew.

CHAPTER 7
LUNCH

The trip to the restaurant forced us to take the interstate which prevented any conversation without screaming in the jeep. I didn't mind. It was nice to take in Mobile while listening to some B-side Van Morrison. It was incredibly relaxing. The city had a nice downtown-scape. It wasn't big, it wasn't small, it was just right. The majority of the interstate ride overlooked some older neighborhoods and the city jail. Not exactly picturesque, but nice. Drew told me before we hit the interstate, and it became incredibly windy and loud, that we'd have to take the Bay Way, aka the express way across Mobile Bay. But first we'd have to go under the city through a tunnel. As we approached it, I looked over and noticed he was talking to himself. Well, his lips were moving but I couldn't hear anything. I quickly yelled, "Are you saying something? I can't hear you." He quickly stopped moving his lips and smiled. "No, I was just thinking to myself. This is a pretty cool little city in a jeep isn't it?" I had to smile too. It was pretty nice. "But you better behave or I'll drop your ass off in that jail." As he yelled 'that jail,' we entered the tunnel and his voice echoed. We both laughed. I knew at that moment this trip was worth taking.

As we pulled up the gravel parking lot to a restaurant atop stilts, you could smell a glorious aroma of spices and fish. The restaurant looked like something out of a visitor's bureau pamphlet. Plastic sharks and marlin with netting adorned the front facade. As he came to rest in a parking spot, he turned to me and said, "I'm so glad you're here. This really means a lot to me." Without a second for me to respond he hopped out of the car and came to my side where he helped me out. "Smells pretty amazing, doesn't it? The food will burn your plate and the beer will freeze your tongue. It's what you get on the gulf coast. I hope you like it."

I looked up at the restaurant and then turned my attention to the running boards along the jeep to assist my ascent to the ground. "I know I'll like it. I couldn't imagine a better place to be for a long weekend." He smiled and started to lead the way. I thought to myself, I hope he didn't read too much into that statement. After all I've been here for less than a half hour and I was already talking like I was considering relocation. Yet, I was starving, my mouth was watering and I certainly wasn't thinking straight. It was after two in the afternoon, the parking lot was only half full, and I was ready for a late lunch with just him.

"We have to get the crab finger appetizer, it's amazing! They pull the legs off of blue crabs, grill'em, and then marinate them in butter. They're served with a tangy, garlic-buttery sauce. And you've got to try one of their micro brews, there's still ice on top of the beer when they bring it out." He seemed more excited than me. I couldn't tell if he was hungry or desperately trying to impress me. "I'm sure it's great, this place looks awesome." As we started to climb the stairs to the restaurant you could feel the cold blasting down the breeze way. "Two?" The hostess asked as Drew nodded. "Would you like to sit on the patio or stay inside?" Drew quipped. "She's a Yankee so we need to keep her indoors or she'll melt." I gave him an eat shit look and the hostess smiled. "Right this way."

The hostess's accent wasn't that strong. She was definitely Southern but there was something still kind of Midwest about it. Drew used to say that the Alabama gulf coast was nothing more than an extension of Florida. It wasn't until you went further north before you entered the Deep South.

As we made our way to the table, I couldn't help but stop and look at the menagerie of pictures on the wall. There were plenty of famous stars who'd come into eat like Matthew McConahay, Hank Aaron, Dixie Carter, all standing with what looked to be the restaurant owner. There were dozens of actors and athletes on the wall, anybody you could think of with a Southern accent.

But more ominous were the pictures of fisherman, covered in oil, laying out boons all over the Gulf of Mexico. The aerials of the buoys stretched all over the once beautiful and bountiful gulf. The pictures of crying women and children on the beach removing tar balls from their feet made my insides turn. The BP oil spill had devastated the area and its residents.

Before we got to our seats, I stopped Drew, "how's the oil spill clean- up going?" He pulled my chair out for me and invited me to sit. "It depends on who you ask. The majority of the surface oil has been removed or burned off. However, sedentary residue continues to wash up on shore. Fisherman go out and catch a lifetime of shrimp, only to have to bring it back and burn it because of petroleum exposure. This has been a sad place to be as the economy has literally been punched in the face." As he sat down you could tell he wasn't completely torn up over the man-made disaster. "Then why do you stay?" He smiled, "partly because I'm making good money attracting people back." He knew my 'huh' face well. "A few months ago, a couple buddies of mine put in a bid to help put together commercials and web-mercials about the resilience of the gulf coast. The natural beauty and the people who make this area what it is. You may have seen them in the airport in Mobile. Hell, you may have seen them in Iowa. They're high quality and powerfully optimistic. I'm proud of them and I think we're playing a role in getting this place back to where it belongs." He grabbed the menu as if he hadn't just confessed an incredibly massive undertaking.

"That's really amazing. That seems to be more your thing, helping people." He looked up and grinned. "But what about your Dad's company, I thought you worked for him?" He put the menu on the table and looked away. "I do. I work for him part of the week, big picture stuff and quality programs. The rest of the time I work with my buddies in the production company. We'll go by the office tomorrow, if you want? And I'll show you both operations. But first, I've got to get some food in your belly. Crab fingers and a beer to start." And just like that he was trying to please me.

He didn't lie about the crab fingers, they were amazing. The beer nearly gave me an ice cream headache. But while the food was good I wanted to know more about his jobs and kids. But he kept asking me questions and didn't allow me time to get any in. "So how's the gang at the TV station? Is the boss lady still running you ragged and making promises she can't keep?" This gave me a chance to vent. After all, that's how we used to talk back in the day. "Everybody's good and frustrated. The ratings have gone up slightly, but not enough to throw a party. June keeps telling me that she wants me to fill in more for Joyce, the main anchor, but nothing changes. I still have those days where I just sit at my desk and do nothing. But the new guy, Cameron-your replacement, he's no you. In fact I don't think he knows who he is." Drew started to smile. "Yeah, I caught a clip of him on the website the other day. He sort of looks like he's talking to a mirror. Pretty big fan of himself, is he?" I couldn't help but giggle. "You have no idea."

"Someone, if I'm not mistaken, is nearing the end of her contract?" I couldn't help but show my disgust. "What's wrong? Is that such a bad thing?

Why do you look so down about leaving that shithole?" I looked outside. "My agent can't get me anything worth anything. He keeps telling me to go on these interviews in cities and stations I don't want to be for practice. Then they offer me a good salary and I turn it down because it's not where I want to go." Drew looked down. "Where do you want to be?" He knows the answer to that question. "I want to go to Chicago. I want a main anchor gig. I want to work at a station that doesn't make excuses all the time." "Do those still exist?" He said in a heartfelt manner. "I don't know, it's frustrating."

"But, I keep talking about me. Tell me about the kids. How are they? Greer is in second grade right? And Eli is in Kindergarten? What's little Walker doing? Is he walking, talking?" Drew's face lit up. "They are all doing well, considering. Greer had a little trouble adjusting to the curriculum but we got her in Sylvan learning center in the afternoon and it's really started to help. Eli is in Tae Kwan do, t-ball, and soccer. I can't keep him busy enough. Thankfully Ms. Eulah is there to help with transportation. Walker is still crawling but has the biggest smile you've ever seen. So it's hard to push him to do anything he doesn't want to do. We'll see them today or tomorrow. They're amazing."

"Who's Ms. 'You-la?'" I slowly annunciated each syllable. It took me a second to realize I had no idea who she was. "Ms. Eulah is my parenting partner. She's our nanny who moved down from Memphis after we all moved here last year. She was Greer and Eli's nanny before we moved to Iowa. I financially convinced her to come help me out. She's a 66 year old woman with a fiery personality. The kids love her and obey everything she says or she threatens to chase them with a switch. The problem is, she's the thorn in my side. If I don't eat enough, she gets on me. If I work too much, she gets on me. If I miss two sporting events in a row, she'll keep on me until I'm the damn coach. I love her to death. She's my other Mom and the kids as well." As those words came out of his mouth, his mood changed and he looked out the window.

"Well, I'm gonna have to meet this Ms. Eulah cause it doesn't look like she's feeding you enough." Drew smiled. Once I completed my Eulah dig, I realized he hadn't finished his first beer. He'd moved his food around his plate but only taken a few bites. Was he starving himself? I wonder if I should say something but I decided not to. I'm not his mom and don't have any right to condemn him. He quickly noticed my observations and began to take huge bites while making comments on how good the food was. I, on the other hand, was doing everything I could to not begin licking my plate and asking for another order.

"That's great to hear. I kind of thought your Mom was watching the kids while you worked?" He looked back out on the water for a second. "That was my initial plan but I realized that my mom was struggling to watch an infant and my nephew. It was just too much on her. Plus, we were constantly fighting over her drinking and smoking. She smokes in the house and it pisses me off. I'm a smoker because I've been breathing those damn fumes all my life. I'm hooked. But I don't want my kids to have the same problem. She starts drinking at five, whether her kid watching duties are over or not. It worries me and she won't admit to having a problem. So it wasn't worth the fight anymore. Plus she's raised her kids, 4 in all. And her new approach to watching kids is putting them in front of the TV for 'educational' shows. That's not what we want for our kids. We wanted them to learn everything and be better than either one of us ever imagined."

It was the first time, he used the word 'we'. I didn't know if I should comment. I was pretty sure he was talking about his wife but some things are best unsaid. "Anyways Ms. Eulah is on the payroll and subsequently follows the guidelines and rules I've set for my kids. I don't have to argue with her on what she did twenty years ago with one of my sisters or me. I'm not perfect, nor do I have a perfect plan, but I want more for my kids. They deserve more than I'll ever be able to give them so I can't stop trying." He spoke with such passion and ferocity. He was adamant those kids were going to have a good life whether it killed him in the process. About that time, I realized how tired his eyes looked. I didn't notice it until he got all worked up. "With coaching sports, having lunch with kids, and working two jobs, when do you sleep?" He looked away again. I probably should have kept that to myself but I was starting to worry about him a little bit. "I sleep fine. I'm sleeping a lot better than I used to. I exercise. I eat right. So, I don't see why anybody needs eight hours of sleep. I go to bed when I'm tired and do what I can when I'm awake."

The last thing he said to me was definitely a verbal cue to drop it. I still wanted to learn more about how he balanced two jobs and three kids, but

I figured I'd wait until later. So instead I hit him up with what the agenda was for the week. "So where are you taking me?" He got so happy when I said that, he seemed glad to be done talking about real life.

"Sweetheart, whatever you want to do, I'm game. It's around 3:30 now, so golf may be a little too hot. Especially since you're a snow bird." He winked. "But we could go to the beach? We could go to my folks' house and swim? We can go to a bar?" Both his beers were just a few sips short of being full, so I had to be careful not to be the only one getting hammered in the afternoon. "I mean I really want to do whatever you want to do. I've got my kids arranged all week but they will be at the house tonight. Which reminds me? Do you want to stay in a hotel or the guest bedroom at the house?" He started to ramble. "I mean I'll put you up near the house. You might be more comfortable? But our guest bedroom's nice and it has its own bathroom. Ms. Eulah will make you eat a huge breakfast and probably make you go to bed at a descent time." I stopped him. "I'll stay with you."

I didn't mean for it to sound like that, but it did, and it was weird. He looked down. He couldn't make eye contact for a second. "That would be great. I'll let you sleep in so you don't screw up your schedule too much." I don't know what I just agreed to, but Drew seemed happy and that made me happy.

CHAPTER 8
HIS HOUSE

After destroying a Tiramisu, which we agreed to share (Drew had one bite) we decided to stop by his house to pick up Walker. Then we'd all go to his Mom's house to get a little sun and swim. The ride to his house was once again loud but peaceful. Both of us had a chance to digest the conversation at lunch. I kept looking over at him through the corner of my eye realizing how attractive he is. And he's just doing everything he can for his kids. He's obviously having some professional success. Honestly, if you didn't know he'd lost his wife a year ago, you would think he was the most eligible bachelor around. An observation even more reinforced when we pulled up to his house.

I say house mildly, it was more of an antebellum dream. There was a fence around the yard made of light pink weathered brick. The front had a circle drive, adjacent to six pillars over-looking the sizable front yard. The house was beautifully landscaped with azaleas that had already bloomed. Magnolia trees with hanging moss lined the side yard and drive way. The garage was in back. Just over the open courtyard, visible from the back of the house, was a cottage. It too was landscaped with a brick walkway that led to the big house and it's gigantic porch on the back with wicker rocking chairs and ceiling fans on full blast. I didn't know what to say to him about the house.

"I thought we were going to your house to get Walker, then your folks." He didn't flinch. "This is my house." Wow!!! What the hell is he doing these days? How much f-ing money does this guy have? It's terrible to find a guy attractive based on his financial stability, but it's a sign of confidence and hard work. If a man works hard to give his family everything they deserve, kudos.

I couldn't say anything as we pulled into his three car garage. Then we made our way up to his house through a covered breeze-way. "Is the cottage the guest house?" I said beaming. "No, that's Ms. Eulah's home. I wanted her to be close but still have some privacy. I've actually never been in there. I had it built shortly after we bought the house and said here's a credit card decorate it in a way that makes you comfortable. But she's adorable. She bought furniture at Big Lots and Wal-Mart. Here she's given an opportunity to get whatever she wants but she still gets what she herself could afford. I love that woman."

"WHELL, I'LL BE DAMNED! DON'T YOU BE BRINGING THAT BEAUTIFUL YOUNG LADY IN THIS HOUSE WITHOUT MS. EULAH GIVING HER A ONCE OVER." Ms. Eulah was short and stocky. She waddled when she walked and wore house dresses like I'd see in old fifties movies. As she made her way to us, I realized she was toting a baby on her hip. "Ms. Eulah, I done told you not to be stalking me from behind that oak tree. I can't be walking in the house with an old black woman all up in my bizness." She stopped in her tracks. "DON'T YOU BE SASSING ME YOU LITTLE UNDERFED SMART ASS! I'LL BE IN YOUR BIZNESS WHENEVER I DAMN WELL WANT TO BE."

You could tell this type of back and forth was a regular thing for these two. They sure did care about each other or they wouldn't have been able to carry on like this without eventually getting into a serious argument. "HMH, YOU ARE ONE FINE LOOKING WHITE WOMAN!" Whenever she talked it sounded like she was yelling. The hearing aids in both ears did not appear to be effective in helping her regulate her own volume. "Who said she was white? I done told you get some glasses." Drew quipped and Eulah was ready. "I KNOW A

WHITE WOMAN FROM 100 YARDS OUT. LOOK
AT THAT TINY LITTLE BEHIND, AIN'T NO
SISTAH GONNA BE ROMPING AROUND WITH
AN ASS DAT SMALL." Drew and I both started
laughing as did Ms. Eulah who promptly gave me a
big sweaty hug. She was breathing so hard, I
thought she might need oxygen. "TAKE YO SON.
HE THINKS HE NEEDS TO EAT FOR BOTH OF
YOU. I DONE TOLD HIM, HE AIN'T GONNA BE
AS FAT AS MS. EULAH, NO HE AIN'T. WELL
COME HERE MS. MOLLY, WE GOT TO GET YOU
A SNACK. YOU LOOKING LIKE YOU'RE
STARVING."

Even though I told Ms. Eulah I had just eaten
lunch, she started dolling out chicken 'n' dumplings
and pouring me a glass of sweet tea so strong, I
thought I would have to chew it. "MS. GREER
WILL EAT THESE DUMPLINGS LIKE NOBODY'S
BIZNESS. I AIN'T NEVER SEEN A LITTLE GIRL
EAT SO MUCH. BUT SHE DON'T GAIN A
POUND. SHE REMINDS ME SO MUCH OF HER
MOM." Drew had disappeared with Walker, I
found out later for a diaper change. "OH HOW I
LOVED THAT LORI. SHE LOVED THEM KIDS SO
MUCH. SHE'S THE ONE THAT HIRED ME IN
MEMPHIS AFTER MY HUSBAND DIED. LORI

AND DREW BECAME MY FAMILY. LOSING HER, WAS LIKE LOSING MY OWN DAUGHTER."

As I started to squirm on the bar stool in the ceramic tiled kitchen, Ms. Eulah noticed. "OH HONEY, DON'T YOU WORRY ABOUT A...YOU BETTER NOT HAVE CHANGED HIS CLOTHES!" She yelled at Drew as he entered the room with Walker in a paisley outfit with matching hat. "DON'T YOU KNOW THAT THIS IS MOBILE ALABAMA, NOT BOSTON MASSATUSETTS. IT IS TOO DARN HOT FOR HIM TO BE WEARING ANYTHING MORE THAN A SHIRT AND A DIAPER." Drew smiled and showed off Walker's new outfit. "Ms. Eulah, he looks homeless when you drag his butt around in nothing but a dirty ole shirt and a soiled diaper." That sent Ms. Eulah off. "THAT BOY AIN'T NEVER IN NO SOILED DIAPER. YOU THINK MS. EULAH GONNA LET HER BABY STAY IN A SOILED DIAPER. I WOULD SLAP YOU UPSIDE THE HEAD IF YOU HADN'T JUST INTRODUCED ME TO THE LOVELY MISS MOLLY. BUT YOU BETTER WATCH YOUR TONGUE WITH ME. SOILED DIAPER, I AM..." She mumbled out of the room carrying Walker. I heard a couple words, "I SHOULD HAVE SLAPPED HIS FACE. MS.

EULAH LEAVE YOU IN A SOILED DIAPER. THE
NERVE YOUR DIDDY GOT."

Drew looked at me and the full bowl of food
and drink in front of me. "Didn't you eat enough at
the restaurant?" I shrugged. "Oh wait, Ms. Eulah
thought you looked hungry." He started to laugh.
"What do I do? Do I have to eat it? I'm stuffed."
Drew grabbed a spoonful and fed me a bite. "Now
you can talk about what you liked about it when she
begins to interrogate you later. I'll dump the rest in
the garbage disposal and hide the evidence.
Remember though, this was the best thing you ever
put in your mouth, ok?" Drew started to dance
around the room, looking in all directions to see if
Eulah was nearby.

Not sooner as he dumped the food, she walked
back in the room. "DON'T YOU LIKE
DUMPLINS?" I quickly responded. "Yes ma'am, I
love the way the biscuits melt in your mouth and
the extra pepper gives it just the right kick." Ms.
Eulah stopped and smiled with Walker stripped
back down to his diaper and a shirt. "THAT IS
SOME GOOD DUMPLINS. I DONE TOLD YOU
DREW SHE WAS HUNGRY." Drew just nodded
his head. "SO WHAT ARE YOU KIDS UP TO
TONIGHT? YOU GOIN TO A MOVIE? YOU

GOIN DANCING?" She started to sway in the kitchen as she mentioned dancing. "We talked about going over to my folks' house to swim and just whatever from there."

I thought Ms. Eulah had heard Drew say the N-word. "YOU DON'T NEED TO BE GOING TO YOUR MAMA'S HOUSE! YOU TWO NEED TO BE OUT! JUST DOING STUFF, TWO GROWN SINGLE PEOPLES SHOULD BE DOING. I GOTS THE BABIES FOR THE NEXT COUPLE OF DAYS. BUT I WANT YOU OUT, PERIOD!" As Drew began to rebuff Ms. Eulah, she started up again. "WHY DON'T YOU ALL GO TO THE BEACH? GET YOU A NICE CONDO. HAVE A PICNIC IN THE SAND. THAT'S WHAT YOU SHOULD BE DOING." Drew stopped her and yelled. "Ms. Eulah, we're friends! I don't want to put Molly in a situation like that."

I kind of liked Ms. Eulah's plan, but Drew destroyed what I thought was happening. I guess we are just friends or maybe he's just not ready. Either way, I felt bad because Drew had to make this declaration and it seemed to hurt him in the process. Again Ms. Eulah stormed away, "I DON'T CARE IF YOU IS JUST FRIENDS, I WANT YOU

OUT OF THIS HOUSE, DOING!" Her voice trailed away again.

Drew was looking at the ground as if someone had just said something incredibly cruel to him. At first, I didn't know what to say. "Hey. I'm up for anything; swimming, beach, drinks, sitting around the house. I came here to hang out with you; I don't care where we are." Drew's shoulders lifted back as if he had been re-energized. "I'll tell you what, tomorrow, we play golf on the beach and get a couple hotel rooms if we get too drunk. Tonight, let's go swim and maybe grab a drink with some friends." I smiled at him. "That sounds perfect!"

Drew grabbed my waist to help me down from the stool. "Let me show you around the house and put your stuff in your room. Oh wait, let me go get your bag." Once I was down, he was gone. And here came Ms. Eulah creeping in the room. "I DONE LOVE THAT BOY TOO MUCH AND I CAN SEES YOU MAKE HIM HAPPY. I AIN'T NEVER SEEN ANYBODY HURT LIKE HE HAS. HE CRIED JUST ABOUT EVERYNIGHT UNTIL A COUPLE MONTHS AGO. HE'D CRY HOLDING THAT BABY. THAT WAS UNTIL A FEW WEEKS AGO WHEN HE SAID HE HAD A FRIEND

COMING INTO TOWN. WHEN I HEARD IT WAS
A GURL, I JUMPED OUT OF MY SHOES."

Drew came back through the glass door in the
kitchen carrying my bag. "Ms. Eulah, I'm sorry I
yelled." Ms. Eulah walked over and gave him a
hug. "YOU AIN'T NEVER GOT TO APOLOGIZE
TO ME. BUT YOU IS GONNA HAVE SOME FUN.
IF IT KILLS ME, YOU IS GONNA HAVE SOME
FUN."

As Drew was about to escort me to my room,
Ms. Eulah chimed in, "YOU GO GET YOUR
TRUNKS AND I'LL WALK THIS LOVELY LADY
TO HER ROOM. I GOT THE BABY IN BED SO
DON'T YOU BE MAKING TOO MUCH NOISE."
So with a quick salute, Drew was gone. We went
the other way. The family room opened out of the
kitchen with the same ceramic tiles on the floor.
The room had a big sectional and a recliner. The TV
was above the fireplace and the ceiling went all the
way to an upstairs banister, where I assumed, were
the bedrooms. The staircase was off the family
room in a small atrium near the front door. As we
started up the stairs she started going again. "HE
WON'T TELL YOU WHAT'S BEEN GOING ON,
BUT I WILL. HE WORKS ALL THE TIME. IF I
DIDN'T TELL HIM TOO, HE WOULDN'T HAVE

NOTHIN TO DO WITH THOSE KIDS. HE TOLD
ME A FEW MONTHS AGO THAT THEY
REMINDED HIM TOO MUCH OF LORI. I TOLD
HIM THAT'S A GOOD THING, BUT I STILL HAD
TO MAKE A SCHEDULE FOR HIM TO SPEND
TIME WITH HIS BABIES. IT AIN'T THAT HE
DON'T LOVE THEM, HE JUST DON'T KNOW
HOW TO BE WITH THEM. BUT THOSE BABIES
NEED A MAMA. MS. EULAH AIN'T NO MAMA
NO MORE. I'M JUST HERE. BUT I'M GETTING
OLD AND THEY NEED A MAMA."

Ms. Eulah had just married us and we hadn't
even kissed. Oh well, old people want to see us all
in relationships. My grandmother was insistent that
if I didn't get married soon, I was going to shrivel
up and turn into an Old Maid. But that wasn't in my
plan, neither was Drew. Anyways I didn't want to
be with somebody who cries all the time. Sure he
looks good and it's obvious that he's successful but I
need somebody that will support 'my' dreams. Be
there for what 'I' want. Even in my head I couldn't
help but sound like a narcissist. But what kind of
Mom could I be? I just looked at Walker for ten
minutes and didn't once even try to hold him. My
motherly instincts were not on point.

When we got to the top of the stairs, Ms. Eulah pointed to the kids rooms. "THERE'S ELI'S AND WALKER'S ROOM. THE PURPLE ONE IS PRINCESS GREERS'S AND THEIR PLAYROOM IS DOWN THE HALL. YOUR ROOM IS RIGHT HERE IN THE CORNER WITH THE VIEW OF MY HOUSE AND THE BACKYARD. BUT DON'T THINK YOU GOT TO SLEEP IN HERE IF YOU DON'T WANT?" She obviously had cracked herself up and was laughing as she put my bag on the bench at the end of the bed. "THE BATHROOM IS RIGHT NEXT TO THE CLOSET. IF YOU NEED TO DO YOUR BIZNESS, NOW MIGHT BE THE BEST TIME BECAUSE IT TAKES HIM LONGER TO GET DRESSED THAN ANY GURL I EVER MET." She started to giggle again and walked back towards the stairs.

I could see why he loved having her around. She said all the things you were thinking of, but didn't have the courage to say. She was an amazing woman and obviously the perfect companion for Drew over the past year. She was completely unselfish, irrevocably in love with this family, and here as long as God kept her on earth. Based on this family's past year, I truly hoped it was for a long, long time. As my thoughts continued to wander on about Ms. Eulah, it hit me; with all that food it might not be a bad idea to use the restroom.

As I walked back into the hallway towards the staircase, I looked at a table centered in the foyer. It had a giant mirror where I checked my hair again and began to look at the numerous pictures. In the middle was a picture of the whole family. It had been taken at church before Walker was born. Greer was in a beautiful flowered print dress, Eli in a suit and tie that seemed tailor-made for his tiny-skinny frame. But standing in the middle were Drew and Lori, arm and arm, smiling. They looked so happy. The whole family together, glad about what the future had in store for them. Even eight or nine months pregnant Lori was still very beautiful. This is their family. I don't fit in this picture. I was speechless and incredibly uncomfortable. What was I doing here? I'm not his wife, these kids' mother, or anything. I'm just a girl that doesn't belong.

CHAPTER 9
NANA'S HOUSE

Ms. Eulah insisted Walker stay behind, and we were told the rest of the kids were in her care for the rest of the day, "SO GO HAVE FUN!" I hoped to see Greer and Eli. We had some good memories of going to church together and playing golf when we all lived in Iowa. But, I guess that would have to wait.

I did love riding in his jeep. I can't describe the freedom of driving around in one of the South's oldest cities with seven speakers gently playing Van Morrison. Moss hung from large oaks and magnolia's canopied the street, creating a natural ceiling above. The city was amazing as was his parent's house. It was white, with four big pillars in front that conjoined two decks overlooking the front yard. There was a circle drive with a garage off to the side with a parked SUV, an *Expedition* I think, resting on a special driveway between the garage and the house. When he opened the door, you could tell dogs lived there, which was quickly reinforced when four dogs charged us at the door. Drew pushed them away with his feet and told them to "shut up". Behind the dogs, a toddler came up to Drew for a big hug. "Where's Nana, Caden? Oh, Caden, this is Molly." I extended my hand, but he just bashfully threw his gigantic brown haired head into Drew's shoulders. Drew motioned for me to follow him.

When we left the gigantic foyer with a sectioned stair case, we walked into his Dad's study. It was a room lined with bookshelves. A plasma TV sat in the corner, a desk with a computer, a rocking chair, and a swoon couch. There was a rug on the floor covering up scored concrete floors. The dining room followed with a big twelve seat oak table, a china cabinet and hutch. It had scored floors with a giant rug. We then walked into the kitchen with brick floors, large ceramic tiles on the counter tops, smaller tiles under the white cabinets, and stainless steel appliances everywhere. On the other side of this beautiful kitchen was Drew's mom, sitting at the kitchen table smoking a cigarette.

"I told you not to smoke with Caden in the house. Just go outside!" She stood up quickly, smiled, and rushed towards me exclaiming, "I have the oven vent on. So you must be Molly." She definitely had the voice of a life-long smoker. I nodded to confirm who I was. "Oh darling you are just cute as a bell. Did you come over to swim?

Can I get you a drink? Do you want beer, a glass of wine?" I looked at Drew, as if to get his permission to drink more beer. "A beer would be great." Drew smiled and nodded. "I don't care Drew, I'm on vacation." His mom quickly responded. "Honey its five o'clock somewhere, I'll get us two. I won't even ask him, he doesn't ever drink anymore." Drew looked away and then engaged back in the conversation. "I'll have a beer too." He said it as if to prove something and his mom's smile got even bigger. "You two get in the pool, its ninety four degrees outside and eighty eight in the pool. I'll throw some beers in the floating cooler."

"I forgot to ask, do you need somewhere to change into your bathing suit?" His mom asked with the garage door opening. "No, I put my suit on at Drew's." She smiled again. "That's a nice house ain't it? He did all the tile work in the kitchen there and here. He had to work fast or Ms. Eulah was going to kick his ass for taking away her kitchen. I'll be right back." I could hear the ice bags popping on the ground as Drew and Caden made their way to the pool. The bay windows in the kitchen overlooked the pool and a massive deck. As I walked outside I couldn't believe my eyes, but there were palm trees in gigantic pots around the pool. As well as deck chairs with umbrellas with gigantic lights in the backyard. "What are the lights for?" I asked Drew who was taking off Caden's shirt; "The basketball and volleyball court."

I started to walk toward the back where stairs led to a fully painted basketball court and volleyball court. There were manicured, colorful shrubs between the deck railing and court. Behind the court, in a lower tier, was a trampoline. "This is where you grew up?" Drew laughed, "No, they built all this crap after I moved out. My sisters were All-American volleyball players, so they built this for them. Get your suit on! It's hot as hell out here." He tossed off his shirt and I could see he was no stranger to the gym. His stomach was not a perfect six pack but he had a well sculpted torso. He was tan and hairy. He had kind of a *Magnum PI* body which was pretty sexy if you like hairy built men. "SPLASH." He dove right in. I wonder if he noticed me staring. "I'm so pasty compared to you. Do you have any sun-block?" With the open of a door his Mom beckoned, "it's right here next to the grill. But you might want to get a starter tan without it." His mom was leathery so I chose not to take her advice.

As I took off my shirt and started to rub sun block on, I reflected on what I looked like in a bathing suit. My stomach was flat, not shapely. My breasts were a good size, a 34C. I had tone legs, not muscular, but I wasn't afraid to undress in front of a guy. I guess I was ok to look at. In the glass windows from the family room near the grill, I noticed him checking me out. Good, I thought, so he does still have those feelings. I don't know what that means but at least I know I can get his attention if I want.

As I walked over to the pool, he dove underwater. His Mom quickly started popping beers and handing them out. "I'm so glad you came down. I think you'll like spending time here. It's hot as hell, but fun." I told her thank you and how I agreed. Drew popped up right next to me with his hair slicked back. "So are you gonna get sloshed tonight?" I gave him an eat shit look. "You just said you were having a beer too. So get your beer and shut your mouth, I'm on vacation." As he turned and headed towards the floating cooler, his Mom piped in. "That a girl, somebody needs to get in his holier than now face. I like you a lot. He needs somebody that will get all over him." As she grinned, I admit I looked startled. Why was I everyone's answer to saving this guy's problems? And what does he need saving from? Having fun? Fun doesn't get you a big house and a successful business? Hell, if anything, I'd take him away from all he's worked for.

"I better start the grill." His mom said as she rushed away from the pool staircase. "Do ya'll want steaks, hamburgers...?" Drew stopped her, "Molly and I are going out tonight. We talked about hooking up with the guys at work. You don't need to bother with cooking anything. " His mom replied, "That'll be great! Ya'll should go out and have some fun. Caden, let's get inside and start getting dinner ready for Papa." The fat little squatty three year old followed his grandmother waddling back inside. He looked like her mini-me.

"Don't you need to let your friends know about tonight or do they just sit on standby in a bar awaiting your potential arrival?" He mumbled something, a frequent problem of his, then stood up and walked over to his oversized cell phone. "Is that your phone? I've never seen one that big!" He started laughing, pushed a button, and brought the phone to his ear. "That's not the first time I've heard that; about my phone of course. What you doing 'bee-atch'? You-going out tonight?" (There was a long pause.) The volume of his voice went down to a whisper. "It's me Drew, I was just, just, you know, saying hello. (Pause) I understand I don't talk like that. (Pause) Yes she's with me, but she's just a friend." He had his back turned to me I would have loved to seen the look on his face. I could tell he was trying to be cool but he just couldn't pull off something that wasn't him. He walked back all fired up. "It looks we'll have a good crowd. I apologize, I don't go out much. It took me a little while to explain to them that I indeed wanted to drink with them in a non-work related function."

Floating in the pool, drinking beer, learning about his dad's company, I started to get a buzz. "You see he gets a portion of the executives first year's salary from the company/client as a professional service fee. It sounds easier than it is. For example he may charge a hundred thousand dollar fee, but the cost of people, resources, and the price of doing business, eats into that more than you might imagine. That's why he has to run a number of assignments so there's overlap with recruiters and researchers." I could see he was proud of the business so I kept egging him on.

"So what's your role in all that? Do you do research, recruit or just bask in the fact that your last name is on the door?" He looked at me as if I had hit on a sore subject. But it didn't stop him from bragging about what he did bring to the table. "I have a fancy title but what I do is recruit new partners, assist in marketing initiatives, and work with the quality function to ensure timely delivery of candidates." I looked at him and made a face, "I got the first part but what does the last part mean?" He smiled, "I built a computer program so that everyone knows the progress of a search. It's like an airport arrival and departure board. It lets you know if we're on time or delayed." I didn't know what to make of it, "so what's your fancy title?" He looked away, "Vice President of Business Intelligence." He started to blush a little bit.

"But you said you were working to get people back to the coast since the oil spill? Are you recruiting people back here?" He got excited again but downplayed it. "No, just the commercials on TV and the web." I was impressed. "And you work all these jobs and have time to play with your kids?" He giggled, "I told you I don't need 8 hours asleep."

CHAPTER 10
DIANA

As I began to prune from drinking and floating, I realized the afternoon had flown by. It was near dinner time and we still had a whole night ahead of us. "Are you about ready to get dressed and meet up with your friends?" He looked panicked. "Oh yeah, I'm sorry, I completely lost track of time. I was just enjoying being here with you." I thought to myself, me too. "We'll have to go back to the house and get you some clothes. Or you can borrow a shirt from one of my sisters?" I was just going to wear what I had on earlier. I didn't see any reason to get too dressed up. However, based on the size of his parent's house, I was sure his sisters would have something suitable. I was lost in thought when a tall beautiful girl walked out the back door and towards the pool.

"So you're Molly? You are pretty!" Drew looked at her with a 'take it down a notch' scorn. "Diana, this is Molly. Molly this is my youngest sister Diana. She's married and has a house of her own, but insists on maintaining a residence here as well." Diana was striking. She had a big smile, with dark skin and hair, extremely buxom on a tiny

120 pound frame. She had to be 5 foot 10. If I'd met her on the street, I would have thought she was a model. "So you came down to hang out with this guy and get him to go out? Actually, make him have some fun?" She laughed at her obviously embarrassed brother. "I just love it down here. I mean it's hot, but we had a great meal, I met Ms. Eulah..." Diana interrupted. "Don't you even try to do something wrong around Ms. Eulah, she'll chew you a new one. One day I was over at their house and Greer was acting up so I was trying to correct her. Ms. Eulah came a charging; (in a poor imitation of Ms. Eulah) don't you be yelling at my babies! Greer knows what she did wrong. When her Diddy gets home, he can spank her. But don't you be yelling at my babies.' At first I was like back up bitch! But then I realized she's pretty much raising them, so I let her be. I actually really like her now. But she loves Drew, he never does anything wrong."

Diana was so energetic when she talked, using her hands and moving all around. I instantly liked her. "Diana, can you get Molly a shirt to borrow? We don't want to stop by the house before we meet up with some people at work." Diana piped in. "I want to go. Where ya'll going?" Drew looked at her. "We're going to Monsoons. You can go, but what about a shirt?" I looked at Diana's figure and wondered if I would be able to fill out one of her tops. "Sure she can borrow one. Molly you want to come up with me and pick out something?" I nodded and jumped out of the pool to grab a towel. Drew followed and I could feel him watching me.

As we entered the backdoor through the family room, I realized his mom kept the house at near tundra temperatures. Again you could smell the cigarette smoke. Diana started to climb the back staircase and I followed. She quickly started in on what was becoming a familiar story. "Molly, you just don't know how happy we are to see you. I mean, we loved Lori. She was good to him and she loved her kids. But Drew's spent a year in mourning. It's time for him to start living again." I had an instant comfort level with Diana. "Can I ask you a question?" She nodded. "Why do I get the impression everybody expects me to come here and marry him?" I was worried, Diana laughed. "No Molly, we're just glad to see him be social again and actually interested in a girl. We used to joke when we were kids that he was gay." She smiled back at me. "I don't think he's gay anymore. I'm not asking you two to get engaged, just take him out and let him have some fun." I had always enjoyed spending time with him. When we reached her closet, she pulled out a shirt that looked too small for me. "You'll look great in this. Lori used to borrow my stuff all the time too. I'm glad you didn't bring anything with you." Diana smiled but her eyes looked sad.

After I cleaned up, put make-up on, Diana and I returned downstairs. I could hear Drew talking to his mom as we got closer. "Don't read too much into this! We're having fun and that's it. Ya'll need to get off my case all the time." His Mom looked up from Drew's scowling directives and smiled at me. "Wow! Don't you look pretty!" I blushed, Drew turned around from his bar stool with his mouth agape. "You look beautiful," he said. Diana ended the adornment. "Are you ready to go?" I nodded. "I'm driving Drew; you drive like an old man. Plus I've got to pick up CJ;" her husband. Drew tried to fire back at her. "Fine, but you and CJ better have a ride home because we're not driving twenty miles to your house!" Diana didn't seem to care about her brother's orders. "Dawn and Aaron are driving us home. They're on the way there now!" Drew looked a little surprised. Dawn was Drew's other sister who also lived in town and had a baby with a guy, Drew didn't like. They became parents but never got married. "I'm not paying for Aaron to get shit faced and ignore his son. Why in the hell did you invite them both?" Diana, still bubbly, was used to her brother's negativity, "Dawn wants to meet Molly too. Plus none of us have been drinking with you in years, so blah! You will have fun tonight and be embarrassed repeatedly with stories of what a horse's ass you are! C'mon Molly, girls in the front, shit head brothers in the back!" And just like that Drew followed like a beat puppy behind us to the jeep.

CHAPTER 11
THE OFFICE

We drove a few miles before Diana pulled into an office parking lot. The building was stucco, one story, with two doors, and small pillars marking the entrances. There were signs on both: "Chandler & Associates;" the other door said "C-suite Productions." Diana turned to the back seat where her brother sat quietly en route to the office. "Do you want to show Molly the office?" Before he could respond she turned to me. "You wouldn't believe what Drew has done to this place in the last year! Let's go inside, everybody who's going out is in there." When we walked in the door, she showed me her desk. Diana was a receptionist, logistics coordinator and researcher. She told me her brother made her come work for the company shortly after he moved to Mobile.

Behind the front office was a conference room and a large office filled with book shelves. Inside sat a man crunched over his keyboard staring at his gigantic computer monitor, wearing a Hawaiian shirt. "Daddy, you want to meet Drew's friend Molly?" He quickly turned and painfully stood up. He was about 6 foot, 280 pounds. He had streaks of grey in his hair but looked incredibly happy when Diana beckoned him. "Molly, it's so nice to meet you. I'm Owen Chandler. Welcome to Mobile, it isn't too hot for you?" I smiled and started to talk when voices started to ring out from the hallway. "Drew, are you hanging out with women? Or are you out shopping with them before catching a ride to the bathhouse?" The voice was baritone and loud. In walked a man in his mid-thirties with a nice blazer and khakis. He had a good body, but was pale as a white sheet. He was laughing after his regular inner office gay joke. "John this is Molly. Molly this is John Wright, he runs this side of the building." I looked at John impressed while he undressed me with his eyes. "N, nic, nice to meet you." His confidence gave way to insecurity. It was kind of cute.

Then another voice rang out, "Drew, did you bring your little friend with you for a frosty beverage?" Suddenly a guy, who obviously spent a lot of time in the gym, walked in with similar attire on. He was loud, obnoxious, but full of life. "This is CJ, he works for John." John didn't let it lie there. "Yeah, but CJ is Drew's brother-in-law, that's why he has a job." CJ made a sarcastic laugh and they all started carrying on in what was now a cramped office. "You guys about ready to go?" Drew was ready to move on, but Diana grabbed me. "Molly you need to see Drew's office and meet the other folks in the office. Plus you have to check out his production company. They've got really cool shit over there! I mean crap. Sorry Dad."

She took me by the arm to an office similar in size to his Dad's. But it was totally different. For one thing, Drew didn't have a chair at his desk. It was tall enough for him to stand and work. Along the outside walls were little desks with chairs behind them. It again resembled the three bear's story. Above the biggest one was a sign that read *Greer-President*. The next size down was a desk with a sign that read *Eli, Co-President*, and finally another one that said *Walker, President Pro-tem*. It was so cute, I couldn't help but smile. The desks had marker holders with sheets of paper, some colored, some completely blank. Their desks were picked up but obviously used. "Why no chair?" I asked Diana. "He never sits down, plus he has back problems. To be honest, he's such a nervous wreck all the time a chair would just get in his way.

Come check out the production side of the building, you'll like Henry and Mark." Diana whisked me through the bullpen where the recruiters and researchers worked in cubicles. Some Diana introduced me too, others we walked right past. There were about eight in all, diligently working, or getting ready to close for the day.

We walked outside and in through another door, which was the production side. The office was very different. It was darker, with four desks in the middle all butted up to each other. At one desk there was a guy completely bald who seemed to resemble a wrestler I remember by the name of "Stone Cold Steve Austen". And the other guy was blond, in fairly good shape, talking to the bald guy about what they were viewing on the giant plasma hovering in the middle of their four desk pod. They both stood up when we walked in. The bald one spoke first, "Hey, Diana. You must be Molly?" It was amazing how everyone knew my name but I had absolutely no clue who they were. So I did my typical nod and shook both of their hands. Diana, ever the tour guide, handled all the introductions.

"This is Mark and Henry, Drew's best friends in the world and his partners in this business. They work all the time but take a look at their toys." We walked into an edit suite superior to anything I had ever seen, with forty-two-inch plasma monitors mounted on the walls. Dark egg crates covered the barren parts for sound buffering. You name it, and there it was; an assortment of high end editing equipment and production stuff. Mark, the bald guy, walked in behind us. "I remember when we were deciding on equipment, we fought day and night. Now we use oversized boxing gloves for disagreements. Drew may have been grieving for the past year but that son of a bitch is still stubborn as hell. It's actually one of his more redeeming qualities." I was really impressed by what they built.

"So where are we going tonight? We've been trying to convince Drew to get drinks since we all moved down here. Unfortunately we're not attractive enough to coerce him." Mark made himself laugh with his own observation. Henry was a bit more reserved. "I am really glad you're here. Not only for Drew but we are desperately in need of a producer and someone who can also talent a few of our projects. It would be nice if we talked before you left." I looked at him a bit taken aback; a job? Is that why I'm here? That kind of changes things. "It's just an idea. I discussed it with Drew a few days ago. But, only if you're interested though?" Henry continued, but my mind was racing with the idea I was on a recruiting trip.

CHAPTER 12
HANGIN OUT

When all ten of us sat down at a table in the bar, the waitress introduced herself then asked "if this would be all on one ticket?" Like clockwork, everyone at the table turned to Drew. Drew looked around the table a little surprised. He then turned towards the waitress, "just one ticket, but don't let any of these assholes order any single malts or twenty year old bottles of wine." His sisters laughed. His friends quickly began ordering high end beers and expensive mixers. This was going to be an expensive night. Yet Drew and I both ordered draft beers on special, a two for one deal. I figured I might want to get used to it since I might be his employee. God that made me mad! But I was here to have a good time and wouldn't let the recent inquiry, completely out of the blue, spoil it.

"So, did you know Molly, that Drew was 290 pounds when he was in 8th grade?" Drew turned his head and my mouth opened in awe as his sister Dawn spoke. Dawn was tall and beautiful with darker hair, and even thinner. She had a baby a few years ago but certainly showed no signs of ever being pregnant. Man, I thought to myself, no wonder his kids are so l, his family is so attractive. Dawn continued, "Yeah, that fat ass used to sit in the house during the summer while my Mom and sisters would go to the pool. He would order Domino's, eat a whole pizza by himself and then lay on my parent's bed watching baseball games."

Drew's friends started in next, while enjoying their free drinks. "Yeah, he may have been fat then, but he wasn't exactly skinny when he started working for his Dad. What did you hit 230? I'm glad you found the gym." His friend John was proud to enter in the conversation. Drew, I could tell, was reeling from the insults. But he didn't get upset; he just smiled and sipped his beer until he decided he needed a break. "I'm gonna go smoke a cigarette so ya'll can continue to talk behind my back and I'll actually not be able to hear it." Everyone laughed a little. "We're just having fun with you."

Drew got up from the table and headed for the front door. After the door shut, the mood changed at the table. Dawn started; "Wow, we can't believe you convinced him to go out tonight. He must really like you." Then his brother-in-law CJ yelled from across the table. "Yeah, it's good to see he likes girls. We were starting to worry he was gonna start playing for the other team; again!" They all laughed, I didn't know what to say.

CJ leaned in with more, "usually, at this time of the night he's at home working. Sending out emails to all of us asking for some quick response, like we all work twenty hours a day. Quite frankly he's become a real horse's ass. But he actually smiled with you earlier, we're impressed." I scanned the crowd at the table, all of whom were staring at me. "I'm glad I could help, but I didn't do anything but show up." I was quickly interrupted by the bald guy Mark, who talked over the barrage of comments. "You don't understand Molly, he never relaxes. He works all the time! He took his wife's insurance money and spent every penny of it. He was so worried he would have nothing left for his kids, which is where Lori had intended it, that he started working constantly. I guess he took a month's vacation when he locked himself in his parents' house. But when he came out, he never stopped. Thankfully, everything he's put his money in; the production company and his Dad's company have all paid huge dividends. Yet he hasn't stopped working day and night. All he thinks about is work. Ms. Eulah started to bring the kids to the office about four months ago, so he wouldn't forget what they looked like. He slowed down a bit, but only slightly." I looked at Mark with a worried face. "Do you think he's ok? I mean, should he be seeing a professional?" Mark quickly responded, "Oh he is, but his therapy has really been in the gym and the schedule with the kids Ms. Eulah made. I wouldn't say he's made a 180, but he's coming around. Shoot, the fact he called you and asked you to come down makes me optimistic. I want to hear him laugh again and make fun of us. That's who he really is."

Drew walked back to the table and everybody shut up. "Should I go back outside? It seems the conversation was livelier when I was gone." He put his hands on my shoulder and looked at his friends and family who all started to grin. "What? Why do you all have stupid looks on your faces? Isn't there something you should be doing?" "Shut the hell up!" His brother in law shouted. "I've already ordered shots!" His sister Diana reached for her brother, "Hand me your phone I need to call Dakota. She'll go crazy when she sees you out at a bar." Dakota was Drew's free spirited sister who lived in Los Angeles and was a professional photographer. She never graduated from college but she was an expert in all degrees of quality marijuana. Drew had spoken of her in the past and referred to her as the 'Fun Bobby' character from *Friends*. She had a tendency to get incredibly wasted and show everyone a good time.

Diana pushed a button on Drew's monstrous phone and started to stare at it. The phone was not only for regular calls but also could make video calls. His sister Dakota with a husky voice said; "Hey bro, what's up?" And then her voice changed to a much higher pitch. "Hey Diana, why are you on Drew's Skype?" Diana started to smile, "Drew has a friend from Iowa, you want to meet her?" Dakota seemed unimpressed. "Sure, what's his name?" Diana made a sound to stop her. "It's a girl and her name is Molly." Dakota didn't realize she was in a group setting so her exasperation made everyone laugh. "Oh my God, are you serious? Is she cute? Are they on a date? Oh my God, I can't believe it!" Diana began laughing as did everybody else at the table. I looked at Drew who couldn't make eye contact with anybody.

"Hi Molly, oh you are pretty! I'm so glad you're hanging out with my brother. He's actually really fun, once you get him drunk!" The phone was now being held in front of my face by Diana. Inside the little screen was another beautiful girl with longer hair, a bit heavier than the other siblings, but had the makings of a clean hippie. "I'm fine Dakota, nice to meet you. Your brother has a pretty amazing phone to be able to make video calls like this." Dakota stopped her. "Oh yeah, we all have them. He thinks it helps us all stay in touch. It is pretty cool. Wow! You are pretty, are you liking Mobile?" I was being questioned by Dakota and being stared at by the occupants at the table. If I hadn't been drinking I would never have been able to continue. "Mobile is wonderful. I like your folk's house, we swam there this afternoon." Dakota boisterously continued. "Oh so you met my Mom? Oh wow! That is awesome! I'm so glad you called, you kids have fun and I'll catch up with you guys later. Bye!" I said bye and the staring competition continued.

Drew didn't do the shot ordered him but instead gave it to me, who certainly didn't need it. But, I was on vacation. After I put my shot glass down, Henry began his inquiry. "So Molly, do you like living in Iowa? Do you enjoy an industry nearing extinction?" Henry was obviously the brains at the table and a TV news cynic. He'd been Drew's producer when he was an investigative reporter in Memphis. They worked together twelve hours a day and drank together every evening. They were inseparable until Drew and his family moved to Iowa and their relationship was reduced by distance. But now they were together again and a force. Throughout the evening, they would suggest something to the other and the receiver in the conversation would make a note in his phone. It seemed like they did this quite often.

"I love Iowa especially in the summer and it's close to my parents in Chicago. As far as the TV dinosaur comment," I smirked at him. "People don't have time to get all their news for the day so TV news is necessary to keep people informed." Henry started to chuckle. "You sound like Drew when he told me he was going back into TV. Both of ya'll are hopeless romantics when it comes to TV news. He's even done some free-lance work here. I can't keep his pretty face, or ego, away from a camera." Drew piped in. "Dude, I just like telling a story every now and again. Hell, I do that shit for minimum wage. It's just for me."

Henry surrendered with a bow. "Sure man, I know. Because you don't work enough hours. It's a good idea for you to be picking up part time work. Anyways, I don't want to talk about you, you narcissist, I want to hear from Molly. So do you still love it though?" I looked at him to see if he was serious, and he obviously was. "I do. I like the control. I like the live TV rush, I mean there's no other profession like it…" Before I could continue Drew's brother-in-law chimed in, "plus you're hot!" He started laughing and his wife hit him hard in the chest. Everyone else at the table cracked up too.

CHAPTER 13
BACK TO HIS HOUSE

It was almost eleven at night and people started to trickle out. The majority of the sarcastic quips were directed at Drew throughout the evening. But as the night went on, Drew started to take it in stride and hit back at people like he used too. I wasn't sure if it was the alcohol or months of bottled up tension. But he was on, and becoming more confident by the minute. Finally he turned to me and asked if I was ready to get out of there. I agreed, since we had such a busy day tomorrow. As I picked up my purse, Drew announced our departure. But the drunken ensemble stopped him and reminded him of his tab responsibilities. We walked up to the bar for the bill, "$484.73," without tip. He looked at me, "they damn sure better have had a good time!" The fire in his eyes was kind of sexy. He paid it and hugged and shook hands with everybody there.

I started to wonder if someone would hit us with some sexual crack. As we were moving away from the table I thought we had escaped an inevitably awkward joke. But leave it his brother in law to end with a finish, "if you pork her, wrap it up! You already got too many kids!" They all started laughing, and we briskly walked out of the bar without ever turning around.

When we got in the jeep, I realized how wonderful a Mobile night could feel. I was pretty drunk and I'm sure Drew had at least a buzz as we drove down the road with "Sex on Fire" by Kings of Leon playing. The day, the night, the drinks had all kind of made me feel a little frisky. I wasn't sure how to play this one. Do I make a move? Do I wait for him? Is he ready? I was wearing jeans, no panties, a tight revealing shirt, and flip flops. He still looked incredible in his jacket, white button up and a blazer. I kind of wanted to stop before we got back to his place and see if there was a way to tell if this night would have a happy ending.

"Is there a place we could park and look at the stars? I mean, it's so beautiful tonight and I'm not really tired yet." That was subtle. I wanted to spend more time with you but not insist upon anything sexual. "Not really," he said. "Not unless we go across the bay. That's about a thirty minute drive. I've probably had more to drink than I should of and it could get a little dangerous if I pushed it." All I could think to say was, "every party has a pooper, party pooper. You're a party pooper." He just grinned and said, "We'll be across the bay tomorrow night. I promise you a sunset and a starlit evening." His response made me want to jump him while he was driving. But instead, I played it cool. I placed my hand on his, resting on top of the gear shift in the center console of the jeep. He flinched at first and then relaxed. I squeezed it a little bit, just to show him I was glad to be there with him.

When we pulled into his garage I noticed the lights were still on in Eulah's cottage. But as we walked up to the back door, the lights turned off. It was obvious we had a pair of eyes watching our every move. When we were in the kitchen he offered me something to drink and some Tylenol for my ensuing hangover, but I declined. I had stuff for headaches in my bag. I was kind of hoping the night wasn't over. He brought over my glass of water and yawned on his way. "Darlin, I need to crash because we do have a lot going on tomorrow. Do you remember where your room is, or do you need me to escort you?" I didn't know how to react; I wanted to say, "I'll just stay in your room so I don't have to find my room. Or, why don't you just show me and tuck me in." I said neither. "I remember where it is. Are you sure you're ready to call it a night?" I stood up and moved towards him. But he backed away. "Yeah, I don't want to be worthless tomorrow when we're out star gazing." So like that, he came over to me, kissed my hand and wished me a good night. Every bit of my being wanted to follow him, but it was obvious that's not what he wanted. Instead, I put my glass in the sink and walked slowly up to my room.

Once I got there, I realized my bed had been turned down. There was a bottled water on the night stand, where a small lamp had been turned on. My bag had been tucked into the closet. This is like staying in a four star hotel. "Thanks Ms. Eulah," I said quietly. I closed the door and began to undress. The shirt I was wearing was pretty comfortable so I chose not change it. When I pulled down my jeans, I was reminded of my lack of undergarments. Shoot, I'm on vacation; I don't need to wear panties. So I jumped into bed. The sheets were a thousand count, or more, because the bed felt like I was in a silk robe. I turned the light off and snuggled into the sheets. When I turned on my side, I started to reflect on the night. I wasn't thinking about all the comments from friends or family, or even the tremendous heat, instead I couldn't stop thinking about what it was like when he hugged me with his hard shoulders pressed up against me. His hands resting under mine in the car or how he looked as he walked over to get us a towel. It all kept replaying in my mind.

As my thoughts started to take the mundane experiences and make them more than that, my right hand slowly proceeded to my stomach. I wondered what he would be doing if we were both in this bed right now. My eyes stayed closed so I could see this dream in full reality. I rubbed my stomach and my hands continued to venture lower. I thought about him on top of me furiously kissing my neck and shoulders. His chest pressed up against mine and his breath heating up the back of my neck. I could feel his legs intertwined with mine, rubbing up and down my calf. I could feel the ferocity of his kisses until we were locked at the mouth. Oh how he pushed so hard on me, with every muscle rippling in his arms and chest. I started to groan and had to put a pillow in my face. Oh how he would grab me and throw me around to put me in perfect position. My insides started to burn. My legs shook. I couldn't get my breath. I started to bite my pillow to keep from screaming out loud. Oh, how I wanted him. How good it would feel! My legs relaxed, my stomach stopped clinching. I pulled the pillow away from my face, took a deep breath in, and realized I didn't want this to be just a friendly visit. I closed my eyes and went to sleep.

CHAPTER 14
LATE NIGHT VISITORS

I don't know if it was hours or minutes later, but I looked up and noticed my door was open. I rolled over on my side and started to squish whatever was in bed with me. I nearly jumped out of bed! The light from the hallway spotlighted a small little blond head smiling back at me. "Hey Mollwy, can I sweep wit you?" His partial speech impediment was so adorable that I couldn't resist. "Eli, is that you?" He smiled and I remembered his face immediately from playing golf with him and his Dad. Not to mention the times he would come up to the TV station so he and his Dad could be together. "Yes, it's me Ewi. Can I sweep wit you? Greer went to her woom and weft me awone." You can't deny anything so precious so I agreed and immediately moved over to make more room for him in the bed.

As I was about to standup and close the door, I realized something. I don't have any pants on! I'm in bed with a five-year-old boy and I don't have any pants on! There has got to be something very illegal about this. My head was pounding from all the alcohol but I had no idea how to obtain pants while keeping Eli out of the loop. My mind was racing but my headache was excruciating. What do I do?

As I sat up and scanned the room for some sort of solution, a shadow appeared in my doorway. Oh please don't let it be Drew and he came up to see me. How could I explain being in bed with his son half naked? I was panicked, then I realized it was Greer in my doorway. She had a blanket and appeared to want something from either Eli or me. "Hi Molly, can I lay down with you and Eli?" If seven years olds can read body language I'm sure she could see something was up. What do I do? Two small children in bed with me and I'm wearing nothing but a shirt. I had to think of something fast and not particularly obvious. What do I do? Got it! "Sure you can both sleep with me, but you've all got to go potty first." Eli was first to react. "It's ok Molwy, I just went potty." Greer was next. "I just went potty too, so can I get in bed with you guys?" Potty distraction, check! What's next?

"How about you guys get me a glass of water from the bathroom, and we'll lay down when you get back. "Ok?"

They both left and I jumped into my closet. But before I knew it, Eli was back in the room. "Do you want a wittle or a wot?" I hid my naked bottom behind the closet door. "A lot, so I can take my medicine." He left and I tore through my suitcase, found a pair of shorts and dashed back to the bed. "Here you go Molly, where's your medicine?" I got back up to locate my Advil, took three out, and swallowed them with my warm glass of water. My heart was racing and I was sweating as the kids got into bed with me. I was a nervous wreck; I was unsure whether I could get back to sleep. When I turned the light out and said good night, I could hear one of the kids faintly snoring. Crisis averted and with a sense of relief, I fell back asleep.

CHAPTER 15
BREAKFAST

The next time I woke, the door was open again and the smell of bacon filled my room. Now that smells like breakfast. My head wasn't hurting, but my stomach was. The only thing I ate for dinner the night before were some appetizers at the restaurant. At the time I wasn't really interested in dinner, but now I was famished. The kids were gone, I wondered if it was all a dream. Oh well, I'll go down and see if Ms. Eulah has something, like that bacon, I can get my hands on.

I changed my shirt, brushed my hair and headed downstairs. But it wasn't Eulah at the stove, it was a sweaty Drew. The kids were seated on the bar stools, the baby in the high chair, all of them mauling pancakes and bacon. Drew turned around and saw me as I approached. "Good morning, I've tried to keep the kids quiet. I'm so sorry if we woke you." He had a spatula in his hand, a hat on backwards, an iPod attached to his arm, and his shorts were wet in the front and back. It was an incredible turn on. "I'm sorry, I'll go get changed as soon as I finish round two for the three little pigs here." Greer and Eli smiled with mouths full of half-digested pancakes and syrup. "Let me get you a cup of coffee. Wait, you don't like coffee, so Ms. Eulah got you some *Mountain Dew*." I stopped him from digging in the refrigerator. "No, coffee sounds good this morning." He nodded. "But thanks for remembering my favorite drink." He pulled off another batch of pancakes and plopped them on the kids' plates. Greer cut Eli's first, then hers. They didn't speak, they just ate.

A few minutes later, Drew raced back in with a pair of shorts and a t-shirt on. His hair was wet, so I assumed he power-showered. "Did you go workout this morning? Why were you so sweaty?" He went back to work on the pancakes. "I wanted to run the alcohol out of my system so I didn't sweat like a stuffed pig on the golf course this morning."

I looked at the clock 7:28. If it wasn't for the kids still in their pajamas I would thought it was much later. "I heard you had some bunk mates last night. I'm sorry. I told them not to bug you before you got here." I sipped on my coffee. "No it was fine; I slept pretty sound with them. Didn't we guys?" Another mouth full of grins and pancakes right back at me. "So you're the chef around here?" He didn't even turn around. "No, Ms. Eulah is the resident cook, but I like to make breakfast for everybody when I can." Baby Walker, was gnawing on a pancake with a juice cup in his other hand. So this is what it's like to have a family. My plate was presented with two nine inch pancakes, with eyes and a smile made out of bacon. The syrup was heated in a pouring bowl. He smiled as he placed my breakfast in front of me. "This looks delicious." The kids started laughing when they saw my pancake face. "Daddy, why did you give Mollwy a pancake face?" Eli roared with laughter. "Molly, you have to take the face off before you eat, or you'll get syrup on the bacon." Greer instructed me as I made for the syrup. "I like syrup on my bacon." The kids laughed again; "So does Daddy. Ha-ha."

CHAPTER 16
GOLF

Ms. Eulah relieved Drew from his parenting duties at around 8:30 and seemed to be whistling with excitement when she heard we were heading to the beach. But unlike yesterday, she didn't comment. She just hugged us both and wished us a wonderful time. Drew said he needed to stop by the office before we went to the golf course. We ran in and out, only to tell his Dad briefly about our plans to go to the beach. The drinking crew from last night was a bit reluctant to ring out their casual insults. Repeatedly they said, "I'm not drinking that much on a Monday ever again." Even though Drew had already run a few miles, he pretended to be as impacted as everybody else. I felt pretty good despite sleeping with little munchkins. At 8:50 we were on our way to the beach.

I asked him to close the windows to differ some of the sound. I wanted to talk to him and see how he was doing without being interrupted by groups of people I didn't know. "So, where are we playing?" Drew turned the radio down and looked up ahead, "it's a course called Rock Creek." My Dad and I used to go there and play when his eye sight was still good. It's not on the beach but about twenty minutes away. If you want to play on the beach, the only option is the gulf state park course. It's not as nice but the views are pretty good of the Back Bay?" He looked good in his sun glasses. But we were talking about golf. "Which is better?" I asked if I really cared. "Rock Creek is phenomenal. But I had to pull some strings to avoid playing in a foursome. The Gulf State Park course might have people in tank tops and ripped up jeans running about, but it is right on the water."

I couldn't tell which one he preferred. So I said the practical thing, to let him know I wasn't all about spending his money like his other friends. "Which is cheaper?" He smiled, "Gulf State Park is probably one tenth the price of Rock Creek, but I don't care about that. I want you to have a great experience. Don't worry about the price." While very chivalrous, his money wasn't what I was about. "I want to go to the Gulf State Park since I'm paying." He looked at me and started to cut me off. "No buts, you've been very generous and I want to bring you out for golf. You buy lunch. I'll get golf." He tried again to explain why he should be the one to pay but I didn't accept his explanation. I just turned the air and radio up in the car and pretended to ignore him until he quit protesting.

"So are you missing anything being away from work today and tomorrow?" I started to smell the salt in the air from the gulf. It was wonderful. "Nothing I can't do later. I purposely rearranged my schedule after you and I talked the first time. It wasn't difficult. Henry and John run each business. I often think that I just get in their way." He was being a bit too humble. "That's not what they say, they told me you came in with new ideas and started pushing stuff that has really paid off. They also say you invested a lot of money in both companies." Drew looked out his window. "Yeah, I wasn't sure that I should have taken so much of Lori's life insurance money and spend it like I did. It caused a lot of sleepless nights. But for some reason it just felt like it was what I was supposed to do."

For the first time, he brought her up. Do I keep going down this path, or do I change subjects? As always, I followed my gut. "So what has it been like, you know, without...?" I couldn't finish my question but he knew what I was talking about. "It's been tough, real tough. I mean, she handled all our finances, our health insurance stuff for Greer's seizure disorder; all the medicine and doctor's visits. She worked with the kids on school work. I mean she did everything. I wonder sometimes why she even kept me around since I apparently wasn't very helpful." He looked out his window again. I couldn't tell if he was getting upset or if he was feeling guilty. "I'm sorry, I don't mean to pry. I'm just concerned about you. I can't imagine anybody handling everything as well as you have." He gave a slight grin. "I can't say I handled it too well. I wasted some of my life ignoring everybody including my kids. I frustrate my friends by refusing to go and do stuff I enjoy. I would mark myself a failure at just about everything. I'm trying now, but I'm not sure how successful I am. It's just not where I expected to be in my life."

I looked over at him astonished he didn't realize how wonderful he was. "I think you're being too hard on yourself. The kids love you, your Dad's company has never done better, and your family has never been closer. What more could you have possibly done?" He got visibly upset and mumbled. "I could have done more." I didn't know what he was talking about so I decided to diffuse the situation and change subjects. "I'm really glad we're enjoying this week together.

Getting out on the golf course with you today will be relaxing and a lot of fun." He half smiled and said "we'll be there in about 20 minutes."

When we got to the clubhouse, I rushed in to pay, so he couldn't stop me. I came back and picked him up in the golf cart. "We need to go rent you some clubs." I nodded no. "I'll just play out of your bag, that way you can help me pick out what club I need." He looked at me for a second and said "ok." At the first hole, I grabbed his driver and whacked the ball 150 yards down the middle. It was probably the best shot of my life. He got excited, "Miss Burke, swinging the big stick I see." I just cockily walked past him and dropped his driver on the ground in front of him. He got up to the tee box and shanked one into the trees on the left. "I haven't played much in a while." I just looked at him and said, "Who cares, we're not on the tour. You can just play from my lie. But since you barely made it past the women's tees, aren't you supposed to play with your zipper down?" He started laughing. "Are you seriously going to hold me to that?" I made a zipping sound. He unzipped and we were off to his ball so he could pick up and play next to me.

The next few holes, we just talked about golf and other mundane subjects. It was fun, but I still really wanted to know more about him emotionally. Not to mention, I still couldn't figure out if we were 'just' friends or is there potential for something more. However, I was scared about upsetting him. So I thought I'd boost his ego first by asking for his advice on TV matters. "I brought down my reel. I thought you wouldn't mind critiquing me a bit on how my anchoring and reporting look?" He grabbed a club out of his bag. "Molly, you know I think you're phenomenal. My criticism might not to do much good, since I'll be hard pressed to identify any weaknesses." I didn't let him off that easy. "Stop kissing up! Just because I'm kicking your ass in golf doesn't mean you need to act like a weenie." He bowed, and with a hand gesture, welcomed me to hit my ball. I was about eighty yards away from the hole and swinging his eight-iron. I asked him if I should hit it hard or soft? He told me to do whatever I thought was necessary since I was 'kicking his ass.'

From my backswing, I smashed the ball high into the air. It was soaring and had the perfect line. Drew was standing next to me, cheering the ball on. As it approached the pin, it looked like it was going to hit it. I started to chant 'c'mon' with Drew. The ball landed just short of the hole, rolled forward, and bam, it went right in! "Oh my God, Oh my God!" I started jumping up and down and Drew was too. I ran over to him and jumped in his arms. He grabbed my waist and butt and jumped up and down with me. In my excitement I looked down at him and kissed him.

In hindsight, I should probably have just jumped up and down and hugged him. But I kissed him hard on the lips. It was the best golf shot of my life and the only thing I could think to do was kiss him. My insides started to boil when we locked lips. My legs squeezed his waist and my hands squeezed the back of his head. He felt so good. He held me tighter not to let me go, and we kept kissing. Such an emotionally charged kiss was something I had never experienced. It wasn't like the casual, he turns his head and you close your eyes then you start to kiss. It was more like a dart to a bulls-eye. You eye your target and hit it hard. Our tongues grasped at each other, he grabbed my butt and pulled me closer to him. I opened one eye to see if his eyes were open, they weren't, and it kept on. After a just a few blissful seconds it ended and he let me down. "Great shot, we need go get your ball out of the cup and head to the next hole." He walked to the cart and left me there. What the hell just happened? Was that a dream? Or did we just make out only for him to leave me hanging? I went from borderline bursting, to feeling like I had just been slapped in the face.

We talked about the shot repeatedly but not the kiss. I didn't know if we ever going too, or if we would just pretend it didn't happen. I kept day dreaming of pulling up to a tree and him grabbing me, then throwing me against the bark. Then he'd tear my clothes away while holding me the same way during the kiss. I could almost feel him thrusting into me while the tree limbs shook above. But he started to keep a distance from me, even in the cart. He hung out his side a little bit more than before; in fact our legs didn't even come close to touching on the white bench.

We bought a cooler of beer before we started and now I really had to pee. "Hey let's go up to these bushes so I can pee." He started to turn the cart. It would be weird if this was the first time I had peed in front of him but before his wife died, his son and I were playing golf and he made a wall for me to pee in some bushes. I walked into the foliage and did my business. When I came back he was sitting there smoking, talking to himself. "Enjoying the dialogue?" He turned to me surprised. "Huh?" I wasn't letting this go. "What were you saying to yourself that looked so interesting?" He looked down and didn't say anything for a few seconds. As I was about to yell an uncomfortable hello, he spoke. "I'm sorry. I shouldn't have done that. That was wrong and I'm sorry." I knew what he was talking about but I thought I'd make light of it. "Don't feel bad, I talk to myself sometimes too. You don't have to be sorry..." He stopped me, "that's not what I mean; I shouldn't have let that happen. I'm sorry I shouldn't have..." I started to walk over to him. "If I remember correctly, I kissed you. You don't have to apologize for anything. If anybody should apologize, it's me. I shouldn't have crossed a line that has obviously made you so uncomfortable." He didn't let me continue.

"It's not a line that's been crossed, it's just, I don't know what to do, I don't know how to act. I don't know what to say, I don't know what I'm supposed to be feeling." I tried to interrupt him but he wouldn't let me. "I like you a lot. I like being close to you even more. But I feel dirty when I think these things. I feel wrong for what I want to do.

I'm married, this isn't right." He was on the verge of tears. I didn't know what to say other than to clear up one important thing. "Drew, you're not married anymore. And what just happened is normal and feelings for another woman are normal. You're not married anymore." He lit another cigarette and suggested we go to the next hole. Nothing accomplished and a lot more awkwardness in the air.

As the day went on, levity returned but so did the humidity. I was sweating just sitting down and my white golf skirt was soaked as was my pink sleeveless polo. His shirt was completely drenched and his butt crack had created a sweat line in his shorts. It was borderline miserable even with the slight ocean breeze. "Are we heading back to your house to change clothes and shower? I'm pretty miserable and I'm not sure I can spend a whole day in a puddle of sweat." He looked at me and then looked out the golf cart as if trying to find his ball. "No, we'll go get a condo and shower up. We'll look for a little store and buy some incredibly touristy clothes. Afterwards, we'll go sit at a tiki bar on the beach and drink frozen, fruity, drinks." It was the first time in a while he was acting incredibly assertive. I liked it. "Sounds great, but I don't want you to spend all that money." He told me to stop worrying about it. But I came up with a plan. "Fine, here's what we'll do. You buy my outfit and I'll buy yours. We won't show each other until we get in the room. Whatever each of us picks out, we wear regardless of how goofy it is." He was laughing again, thank God. "I like that plan, but what if I get you a string bikini, are you going to wear it regardless?" I liked where his head was at. "The rules are the rules."

CHAPTER 17
DRESSED FOR THE NIGHT

We walked into the tackiest souvenir shop that I'd ever been in. Every article of clothing appeared too colorful and potentially flammable. I quickly located a shirt with a hot pink flamingo on the back. I also picked up some white see through linen shorts, I thought would be a riot, and flip flops with a floral print. I rushed to the register so he wouldn't be able to see his evening apparel. As I swiped my debit card, I noticed him hiding in an aisle waiting for me to make my exit. "I'm going to the car; I'll meet you out there." He nodded and stared me down as I crossed the threshold of the store. A minute later he threw his bag in the back, sealed at the top. "Am I gonna like the outfit?" He smiled, "maybe. I'm sure the boys will." Oh, something kind of sexy and tacky; what a perfect way to dress the day away.

As we made it to the strip, that uncomfortable conversation started to surface when he mentioned staying down here tonight. One room or two? "I'm not sure we can get a condo for just one night, but we could get a couple rooms at a hotel? I'm just trying to think what's on the strip that's near everything you'll probably want to see." I was looking at the giant condominiums up and down the street. They were all so large you it was hard to imagine there was actually a beach on the other side. "Shoot Drew, we could stay at a dive, I don't care. We'll probably be so drunk when we get in tonight it won't matter." He laughed a little. "Yeah, but I'm not staying in a dive, passed out or fully sober." I forgot he was a little pretty girl. It was now two in the afternoon. We both had a couple beers on the course and held each other's fashion futures in our hands. Soon we would be in a place where anything could happen, if only he would let it.

"Sir, we don't have any rooms, but we do have a suite available?" Drew looked at me, excited. "How many bedrooms?" He looked down at his computer after staring at me. "It's got one bedroom but a spacious living area with a fold out couch." The guy behind the counter winked at me and I turned to Drew who was very happy with the proposition. "Is that alright if I crash on the couch and you have your own room?" I wanted to say no, you're not paying for this and then sleeping on some hotel couch, but I instead I wimped out. "That's fine; we'll draw straws on who gets the bed." He told me that was a deal and we carried our souvenir bags over to the elevator and headed to the top floor.

The room was superb, spacious, with a kitchen, a couch, a recliner, a plasma TV on the wall and a desk. All of the colors in the room were pastels, not gaudy but beachy. The bathroom was also lavish with a Jacuzzi tub. The bedroom included a California King Sized bed, a bench at the end, and a plasma mounted on the wall. "Oh Drew, this is beautiful. Who's getting in the shower first?" "You can, I need to call Eulah and let her know I won't be home tonight. But do you want me to get you something to drink you can enjoy in the tub?" Oh what an excellent idea I thought to myself. "Sure, is there somewhere nearby?" He looked around the room and found the information binder. On the second page listed room service and the numerous drinks that could be delivered. "Hop in the tub, I'll surprise you with something fruity when you get out." I looked a little heartbroken and sounded a little spoiled. "Could you bring it into the bath for me, when it gets here?" Before he could respond I rushed into the bathroom and started the tub. Jacuzzi jets and bubbles, this was going to be wonderful.

CHAPTER 18
DATE NIGHT

As the water ran, I examined my naked body in the mirror. Why did I keep checking myself out? It was as if I was trying to convince myself I was good enough for him. As the water approached the cut-off point, I gingerly tip toed into the bath. It was scolding hot and I had been sweating all day, not the best of combinations. But I'd forgotten to pour in the bubble bath. The Jacuzzi jets would suffice. The jets were positioned perfectly; along my lower back, my feet, my shoulders, and there was one that kept getting fresh with me. But I didn't mind, it may be the only action I get this week I don't initiate myself. A knock at the door came, "your drink is here." The jets and the motion of the water seemed to cover me up well enough that he was only going to get a blurry peak of me.

"C'mon in! Just close your eyes I don't want to scare you off!" The door handle creaked open and the Pina Colada entered first. Behind the drink was a blindfolded Drew, asking for directions to the tub. I couldn't help but laugh. "You really are a gentleman, aren't you?" He ignored me, "your drink my lady. If you'd be so kind to guide me to your location?" I was laughing as he dragged his feet across the floor to me. I leapt out of the tub, with my boobs hovering above the water. He wasn't looking, so my discretion didn't matter. "Here you go." He gently placed my drink beside me and then held out his hand, "my tip." I thought about jumping up and kissing him or tearing his blind fold off and pulling him in, but instead I aired on the side of sarcasm. "Here's one, don't walk in a bathroom with wet floors blindfolded!" I cracked myself up and he grinned as he made his way to the door which he found with ease. Was he completely blindfolded? I wonder now. I don't care. I preferred he got in with me anyways.

As I let the water drain and sipped the last few ounces of my drink, I realized I had no clothes. I could ask him to bring them to the door or I could have some fun with him. Fun seemed to be the better option. I took the big towel and wrapped my hair up. Then I grabbed the smaller towel, most likely the floor matt, and wrapped my body up in it. It covered my front fairly well, but my back was a bit more revealing. I opened the door and turned in both directions to find him. He was on the recliner smiling as he watched a movie on TV. "Hey where did you put my new outfit?" He looked over at me and nearly dropped his beer. "I, I um, I have it on the table. I'll bring it to you." Let the fun begin. "No, I'll get it, you relax. It's your turn to shower anyways."

I walked over to the bag and grabbed it. Part of me wanted to drop it and really give him a show but I thought that was really slutty. So I picked it up and said thank you. "You better not have gotten me something hideous. After all you'll look like the asshole if I'm wearing something ridiculous." He was staring at me. I turned and walked towards the bedroom, I felt his eyes burning through my body. He was looking and he was thinking. My little trick may have gotten him to reconsider this two room thing. I'm sure the bottom of my ass was showing, I could see it in the mirror when I walked by one in the bedroom. I thought to myself, "You can help me get dressed if you'd like." But again too slutty. Man I must have been unbelievably horny. I said nothing and closed the door behind me.

When I opened the bag, I realized he didn't understand the concept of buying incredibly hideous outfits because what he picked out was beautiful. He had bought another bikini, this one with vertical stripes with hints of light and dark blue. The suit was not nearly as revealing as others

I owned. It was classy and elegant. I assumed these were my undergarments. He also got me a beautiful sundress with a pattern that seemed to come from the same print as the bikini. It was subtle and beautiful. Even the flip flops were something I would have picked out at the store. Now I feel like a total bitch, I've got to run to a store and pick him something out that's better. Wow, he knew my colors and my taste and I just made fun of him with an atrocious outfit. His shower was running, I wondered if I had time to sneak to a store and buy him something else. And like that, he was done.

"Very nice!" He yelled from inside the bathroom and started to laugh a little bit. Man this was embarrassing. I only had my bottoms on but I began to run for the door. I've got to stop this. "My favorite colors, how did you know?" I began opening the door but he yelled out, "I love it. Get dressed. I got to get some food in you." And just like that I let go of the door handle and returned to my beautiful outfit. He was going to look like a fool and I would look incredible. Once again I felt so guilty. Why did he do this to me? Who am I kidding? Why did I do this to myself? Wait a second, why do I care? I live in Iowa, and my life is fine the way it is. This is over in twenty four hours. I've got to stop reading too much into all this. I think the family and friend talk has started to consume me. It doesn't matter what happens tonight or tomorrow, it's all over tomorrow night.

"You look incredible! Wow!" He came up to me and grabbed my waist and began to check me out and up and down. "I didn't know what size to get you, so I aired on the side of hot!" He didn't have his shirt on, just his shorts that were a little more revealing than I had anticipated. As I started to giggle, he quickly became embarrassed and covered his crotch. "I guess I should have gotten you some boxers with those shorts." We both started to laugh as he walked away covering himself with his hands. He grabbed his shirt and threw it on. It was hideous! But he still looked good in it. I liked that he wasn't wearing an undershirt which he always did.

"So drinks? Drinks and food? Drinks, food and drinks?" I told him wherever was fine with me. Arm and arm, he escorted me to the elevator. I looked back at the bed, the sanctuary that could be ours tonight. What was I going to have to do to convince him that we could be together? What kind of move would I have to make for him touch me?

How did I get him to realize he wasn't married and we were together at this moment, and this moment is all that mattered?

Ten minutes later, we sat down at a tiki bar, covered with fans and a straw roof. The host, who brought us to our seats, had a kind, but sarcastic word to say about Drew's shirt. But Drew just made light of it and said that I bought it for him. "I would wear anything this lovely lady bought for me as well." He bowed and made his exit. "Everybody in the south is so polite and fun loving. It's like a vacation all the time?" He looked out towards the water. "I've never cared for the beach very much. The kids always want to come down so I sponsor trips with their aunts. The beach is beautiful and peaceful but it's just not my thing. I like walking from one museum to another, checking out all these amazing man made edifices and their spectacular detail."

I looked at him. "Then you would have loved being with me when I did a semester in France. That's all we did. We'd go to class and then spend the afternoons getting lost in Paris. On the weekends, we'd travel all over Europe staying in hostels just taking in everything we could." "I envy you," he said. "The last time I was in Europe, we were like the Griswold's lost in a tourism time warp. It was Euro Disney and American restaurants. Traveling with my parents is not the most enlightening experience, but they usually pay, so that's nice." I looked at him, "I guess you could fit the bill now." He looked back out at the beach. "You know before we lost Lori, my Dad was nearly bankrupt. The economy had crushed his business and he wasn't able to make payroll. He couldn't even borrow any more money. Even his house had a lean on it. That's why I went to work at the TV station, I needed money. Lori and I were barely hanging on. Greer's medical bills were in default, our house, our cars; everything was on the verge of foreclosure or repossession. I even did a small stint working at a warehouse to make enough money to pay for our living expenses. I loaded boxes all night long, and took a short nap, then went back to work for my Dad in the morning."

He paused for a second and then continued. "When she died, I didn't have enough money or credit to bury her. Neither did my family. I remember sitting in the mortuary, having the price of everything listed off, wondering if I was going to have to tell them "no" because I couldn't afford it. Thankfully my Dad's Mom, my Grandmother, loaned me ten thousand dollars so I could pay for the funeral she deserved. Hopefully one our kids will remember." I looked at him in shock I had no idea everything was so bad, he was always so pleasant and on top of the world. "That's probably one of the biggest things I regret about my marriage, is that I was never able to give her anything she deserved. I'm in pretty good financial shape now but only because she put me and the kids there. She always did much more for me than I ever did for her."

He was tearing up, but so was I. God, He loved her so much. He felt like a failure, who had subsequently conquered everything he put his sights on. "She deserved a lot more than me." I stopped him there. "You wait a second. Look at what you've done. You're raising three kids by yourself. You run two companies, and before then you swallowed your pride and loaded boxes at night to make ends meet. I would say you've done a lot, and you did a lot for her. I know you still care for her, but don't feel guilty for what you haven't done. You're very special." Our drinks arrived and both us sat there looking at them with tears running down our faces.

We sat there in silence, sipping on our daiquiris for a while, listening to Jimmy Buffet playing in the background. He broke the tension; "I've always hated Jimmy Buffet. It's not that I don't think he's talented, it's just I don't know why he's so popular. He's a cult icon in Florida and Alabama." I started to smile at him. "Frankly, I've never cared for him, but his music is the perfect backbeat to a few drinks on the beach." Drew nodded because he knew I was right. "Are we star gazing on the beach or finding a restaurant with a patio?" I smiled at him. "I'm up for anything." He just shrugged his shoulders and looked out at the water with his tear-stained cheeks exposed.

"Can I ask you something?" He leaned across the table to indicate I had his full attention. "Have you dated any in the past year?" Quickly he leaned back in his chair and breathed back hard. "Yes and no. I haven't asked anybody out, if that's what you're wondering? My friends love to invite me to dinner with their wives who suspiciously bring a female tag along no one tells me about until I get there. I mean, I appreciate what they're doing, but it's always awkward. I'm fairly certain my professional success is always the subject to trigger the encounter. Often that's all my "would be dates" want to talk about. I usually counter with my 'three honoree kids, who can't be contained.' Their typical response with a smile is, 'but at least you have a nanny.'"

I had to keep this probe going as it could determine the next few hours of my life, if not longer. "Do you want to date?" Again, another deep breath. "Yes." A long pause. "The last time I was in Memphis letting the kids spend time with Lori's parents, her Mom asked me the same question. I told her what I'll tell you now. I do, but the person has to have something special about them. I don't want a Lori replacement. I want somebody that makes me feel a love I've never felt before. Not better or worse, but different. I can't be with somebody I compare her too. There's no comparison, she was my life for twelve years. I can't act like that didn't happen. The only similarity I look for is friendship and a complimentary personality. At the end of my explanation, I asked her for permission." I had to interrupt, "you asked your mother in law for permission to date?" He looked at me somberly. "I did, and she just asked me to find somebody who would love my kids nearly as much as Lori did." His mouth was hard, but a grin broke out. "Maybe someone who'd be willing to take in a few bunk mates in the middle of the night!" We both started laughing.

"Where do you want to go eat?" I thought my inquiry needed one last question. "I don't know, let me ask you this first?" He got closer to me. "Are we going on a date or are we just having dinner?" He pulled his sunglasses off his head and cleaned them with his horrendous shirt. I kept looking at him and he kept cleaning his glasses. Then he stood up and grabbed the check. "Would you be so kind to be my date for dinner tonight?" I blushed. He was formal and so incredibly handsome. "It depends." His mouth dropped. "Are you going to wear that repugnant shirt?" We both laughed and he handed the waiter a hundred dollar bill for our forty dollar check and told him good luck! The waiter yelled back, "No sir, I wish you good luck." He gave Drew thumbs up and we walked out the door.

We chose a seafood restaurant within walking distance of the tiki bar. It was quaint and elegant. Along the way, we stopped at a souvenir shop and I bought him a not so hideous shirt. He grabbed my hand as we walked out of the store and held it tightly all the way to the restaurant. We did stop along the way so he could give his shirt to a homeless guy sitting on the corner.

When we sat down, he was the first to speak, "If I haven't said this before now, I apologize, you look beautiful." He was staring at me and I was beet red; thankfully, my sunburn helped cover my true reaction. "You look pretty good yourself. By the way, I never did ask you why you stopped drinking. Every one of your family and friends keeps commenting you never drink anymore." He put his napkin on his lap. "Two reasons. As a single parent I never want to be in a situation if I ever had to rush one of my children to the hospital or something bad happened, I would be too drunk to do the right thing. Or in any way harm them in the car of a drunk driver. They've already lost one parent, two was too many. Secondly, I don't drink when I'm depressed. When I was in college, I had shoulder surgery my freshman year and the doctor said I would probably never play baseball again. The news was devastating to me since playing baseball, specifically pitching, was all I knew. So I started drinking all the time; morning, noon, and night. If I wasn't an alcoholic, I don't know what an alcoholic is. The drinking got so bad that one night I got in a huge fight with my Dad who kicked me out of the house afterwards. I ran to Memphis, where I moved into my grandparents' house. I locked myself in one of their bedrooms and read about one hundred books; a book a day. I only left the room to smoke. After I got my life back on track and played baseball again, I vowed to never drink to cope. I only drink when I'm looking to have a good time." I sat there astonished. "How did I not know any of these things about you? I always thought you coasted on rich parents and had a fairly good life." He stopped me. "I did have a good life. I mean, I do have a good life. Each moment I went backwards was an experience that helped me move forward. My dad is probably my best friend. My grandparents are my life, which is why I bought them a house, a new car, when I had the means to do it. Shoot they almost kicked me out of the house when I refused to leave the house for a month. Instead they inspired me. Those moments, though painful, shaped who I am. It hurt, and I cried a lot, but they made me better." I started to tear up again. I was falling in love with this guy not by what he had done but by what he had overcome.

CHAPTER 19
DESSERT

The meal was superb. The aperitifs with dessert were amazing and it was closing in on the end of the evening. "So what's next?" He laughed at me and said, "You are insatiable. I'm a little drunk and I've had a wonderful time. What are you in the mood for now?" Though I was a little bloated from all the drinks and food, I wanted to be with him now more than ever. "We could go for a walk on the beach?" I half smiled, it wasn't that I didn't want to go for a walk but I was hoping he'd say let's go back to the room and see what happens. But instead I said, "That sounds like a great idea. We can walk off dinner." He motioned to the waiter and asked for the check and couple drinks that we could carry out with us. He slipped a twenty in the waiter's shirt pocket who said there were some kids plastic cups he could conceal some walkers for us. Arm in arm, with drinks in hand, we made for the beach.

"What do you want now?" I said as we kicked sand on the water's edge. "I want to be happy. I want to be with people that make me happy." I stopped him. "Do I make you happy?" He looked down at me, he was nearly a foot taller than me. "You make me very happy, but…" I stopped him and pulled his face down to my level and kissed him.

His response was a bit more timid than before. After all, the excitement from my amazing golf shot wasn't driving the moment. I let go of him and he cracked a very scared smile. "What's wrong? Can't you just enjoy being here with me?" I was pretty drunk and probably saying more than I wanted. "It's not that. It's just I suspect I know where this is going and it's been a really long time for me and I don't know…" I pulled him down for another kiss, this time he grabbed me and pulled me close. There was no doubt he liked what was happening as I could feel him. But again he stopped it, and grabbed my arms and pushed me away. "I just don't know if I can do this." Now I was starting to get annoyed. "You like me? You find me attractive? What's stopping you? It's not me, I want this to happen." He walked past me. "It's not that simple, I just…" I stomped my feet. "Stop walking away from me and talk to me! You keep giving me mixed signals and you keep turning me on and off! Why?! You say you want to be happy, well let me make you happy." He yelled back. "I can't, dammit! I've dreamed of this moment a thousand times and every time I don't stop." "So," I said. "Why does it have to stop now?" Again he yelled. "Because I dreamed about this moment while Lori was still alive! I wanted you so bad that I thought about you when I should have been thinking about her!" He kicked his feet and I could hear a whimper in his voice. "I've loved you for years, when I should have loved her. Now she's gone and all these dreams are coming true and the guilt is eating me up inside."

Not what I was expecting to hear. I was speechless. He was sitting in the sand now, looking up at the moon. The light showed the tears rolling down his face. I just didn't have the words for this moment but it couldn't end on this note. There was more to say. There must be something so right about all this or it wouldn't have happened. But how do you tell a widower it's ok to have had thoughts about another woman while he was still married. We both just sat in the sand for what felt like eternity.

"I really don't know what to say. I don't know how to take away what you're feeling inside. All I can say is in the past two days, I've learned more about you, than I've ever learned about anyone in my life. You left yourself completely vulnerable and because of that I thank you for trusting me. I care about you a lot. I know my actions over the past year didn't show that, but I've thought about you. While I didn't start out this week having these kinds of feelings for you, I do now. And I don't want to hold them back anymore." I reached for his shoulder and peered up into his eyes. "If you're not ready for an intimate relationship, I understand. If I leave tomorrow with just memories of what we've experienced together, I won't be happy about that, but I'll understand. But at the end of all this, I want you to know that I want you to be happy. Whether you're happy with me or someone else. You deserve that. I don't care if tragic moments shaped you, I don't want you to continue stocking up stories of heart ache and remorse. I want you to have fun. Since I got here everybody said how much they missed your smile and your laugh. I want you to laugh again…" Now I was crying. "It's time something wonderful happened to you only because you did nothing more than be you."

He leaned down with tears in his eyes and kissed me. It was so delicate but forceful. He pushed his forehead up against mine and looked me straight in the eyes and said "I don't want this night to end either."

CHAPTER 20
NIGHTCAP

We pulled up into the parking lot of the hotel and he looked at me. "Thank you for everything. Thank you for coming down. Thank you for looking so amazing in that outfit." I did a cry laugh, he looked out the windshield. "I'm ready to go to our room now." He said the last phrase with such intensity that the emotional rollercoaster the night had become was now a distant memory. I looked at him with expectations and excitement.

When we walked in the room, I noticed a bottle of chilled champagne on the table with two glasses beside it. "Can I pour you a glass?" I smiled at him and suddenly became so insecure about what I expected was on the verge of happening. He poured a glass of champagne and walked over to me and kissed me on the cheek. "You do look stunning tonight." He started to kiss my neck but then it hit me, dammit, I have to pee! How do you stop this moment? We've already had so many near misses. Can I hold it in? Oh shit I was distracted and he noticed. "I'm sorry, but our timing maybe off again." He looked at me bewildered. "I really have to pee." He started laughing. "I do to, but I was afraid to say anything." He kept on giggling as I ran to the bathroom. After I washed up, I decided I would come back in just the bikini he bought. But as I opened the door, he rushed by me and lifted the seat for himself. "I'm sorry but I was about to burst too."

So here I was standing in the door of the bathroom while I watched him pee. I had just seen his penis and not in the context I had expected. The mood wasn't gone but it had definitely changed. He washed his hands and came up to me and said, "We shouldn't force this. It's after midnight now and if and when this is going to happen, it needs to be the right time for it. Do you think we could crash and see what happens tomorrow?" I looked up at him and agreed. It wasn't that I didn't want him anymore, quite the contrary. But if this was going to be something more than whatever it was, the mood was gone. "Ok, but you're not sleeping on that couch, let's get in bed."

He pulled off his shirt and I removed my bikini top. I grabbed his shirt and put it on. I did it right in front of him like I had exposed myself a thousand times to him. But he didn't say a word. He pulled down my side of the bed and got in on the other. I rolled over onto his chest and put my hand on his stomach. My touch had visually turned him on but he didn't say anything. He kissed my forehead and told me good night. He was so warm and I liked the way it felt to be close to him. It was so comfortable, so perfect. I felt so relaxed; I drifted easily off to sleep.

CHAPTER 21
THE NEXT DAY

I woke to the smell of coffee and the clanging of steel pans. Breakfast had arrived and he was already beginning his day. I walked into the living room as he was preparing our settings, still shirtless with his hair disheveled. "Good morning." He walked over to me and grabbed my waist and kissed me. I kept my mouth shut like a steel trap to hide my horrendous morning breath. "What time is it?" I asked. "It's 9:30. This is the latest I've slept in a long time." I looked at the food and then back at him. "I'm glad I bring the laziness out in you." He giggled a bit and we sat down to eat a feast.

Afterwards, he told me he was going down for a smoke and asked if he could borrow his shirt back. Again, casually, I stripped down to my bare chest and handed him his shirt. This time he stared at me the whole time. He kissed me again and held me very close. I still had no top on but I was much too full for this to go any further. But, that wasn't his intent, or mine. I think we both wanted to show each other how comfortable we were around each other; it did feel good to be close. I actually slept harder the night before than I had in years. He left the room but gave me a kiss on the cheek before he left. It was surreal. I've been in this situation before with the night after un-comfortableness, but there wasn't anything weird about it. Maybe, because there was no sex. Either way, I was going to maintain this openness. I had time to go to the bathroom and get in the shower. But I made a decision to purposely leave the door open. He could come in if he wants I thought. I want to take this to another level, I want to be with him.

But he didn't come in the shower. He stayed in the living room waiting for my departure. When I walked out, holding the towel over me, not covering up, he mentioned he bought some toiletries and they were on the sink. He then told me he was getting in the shower next. The door was open as he started the water. So he failed my test and now he wanted to see if I would pass his. Man I thought, I continue to make all the first moves. Why stop now?

I pulled the curtain back and looked him over top to bottom. He was lathering soap in his hands and was preparing to wash up. I stepped in the shower; neither of us said a word. He put the soap down and reached for my hands and kissed me. It was so delicate. He pulled away from me still holding my hands, and scanned my whole body. It was very special but at the same time humbling. He came up against me again and kissed me. He was definitely in the mood and the passion turned into fury that went from the shower to the bedroom.

We both fell asleep on the floor, wrapped in the comforter in front of the bed. The room looked like rock stars had thrown a party. It had been a long time for him. I could tell by his countless attempts to stay in the game after he had scored. (Pardon the sports analogy.) The sex was beautiful. That's the only way I know how to describe it. It was emotional, it was deep, and we both touched each other in ways that we both wanted. We never spoke a word. It was innocent but filled with curious inhibitions bursting in every movement we shared.

The phone rang shortly after we dozed off. Drew got up to answer it and realized it was time to check-out. We also needed to get back to Mobile so I could pack my stuff and get to the airport. The airport! Oh my, I'm leaving today. And everything has just started. I'm not ready to go home yet. This can't be it! This can't be over! We've been through so much. It's only been three days that I'll never forget nor ones that I ever want to end. "We need to get dressed and head back." He knelt down and kissed me. I reached for him and pulled him on top of me. Our bodies once again in a perfect embrace. I knew the moment I got dressed this wasn't going to happen again. I held him so tight and he lifted his head to look at me. "What's wrong baby? Are you alright?" Now it was my turn to cry. "I just don't want today to end. I want to stay here with you." He mumbled something and began to tear up. "We're just going to the car; you're not getting rid of me yet."

When we reached the car, we both fell silent. It wasn't the uncomfortable, we just had sex, it was obvious the clock was our worst enemy and we could feel each tick. "Do you want to grab some lunch on the way back or do you want to head straight to the house?" I was feeling a little sick to my stomach. I didn't know if it was breakfast, the alcohol, or the fact that this was all going to end in four hours. "I'm fine, I don't really want anything. Hey, how much does it cost to change a flight to a later time?" Drew smiled. "I'm sorry sweetie. Your flight is the last one out of Mobile for the day. I intentionally did that so we could spend more time together." I looked out my window. I wanted to cry. Why was I so upset? It was just sex. It was just a fun couple of days. Why was I punishing myself? "But we'll get together soon, I promise." He turned the radio up and we cruised across the bay way back into Mobile. In what seemed like brief moments, we were in his garage getting out of the jeep.

CHAPTER 22
OPPORTUNITY CALLS

We walked in the back door, and noticed a note on the island in the kitchen. "The babies and I are at the park and then we're going to Greer's doctor appointment. There's some chili in the fridge, you kids eat something. If I don't get to see Molly before she leaves, please tell her I look forward to her next visit. Love, Eulah." I smiled, "My next visit, and when will that be?" Drew started to walk towards the fridge. "How about next week?" I knew he was serious, but that can't work. "Drew, you know you can't fly me down on all my days off. Not only will you go broke, but..." Drew straightened up and looked at me. "I have plenty of money and I could fly you down every weekend for a hundred years and still have money left over. Let's not talk about my financial well- being, let's talk about what you want?" I looked down at the letter on the island. "I want to see you more, I want to be around you more, but I'm a TV person. Mike always says we're migrants, we come and go." Drew looked back into the fridge.

"Are you still sleeping with Mike?" Wow! That came out of left field I thought. He better not be getting jealous, he doesn't own me. I stared at him with an eat shit look. "That's not fair." He grabbed water and brought one over to me and opened it up. "You're right it's not, I'm sorry. It's just, I'm not looking for some fling, an occasional sexual encounter, I want more. I've thought about you for a long time, you're good qualities, and your flaws, which are very few…" He caught himself. "I want to be with you if you want to be with me. How we define that can come in time. Don't think I'm looking for a commitment, but instead effort. If you care about me, and I care about you, shouldn't we give each other every opportunity to see if that's the way it supposed to be?" I don't think I could have said it any better. So I walked over to him kissed him. He pressed on me and I pushed him back into his room. With just couple hours left before my departure, we made love one more time. This time it was even more special. We were in his house and we both knew we had to try.

We lay together for a while and I asked him if he was thirsty? He said "yes," so I went to get us both something to drink. As I made my way to the kitchen the back door opened. I was just wearing Drew's shirt and nothing else. "OH LAWDY! MY APOLOGIES MISS MOLLY." She was giggling as she spoke. "I'LL JUST BUY LITTLE WALKER ANOTHER PASSIFIER, OH LAWDY, LETS ME GET OUT YOU KIDS WAY." I could still hear her giggling as she walked from the back door to her car. I know I was blood red in the face; how embarrassing.

I grabbed the water and made my way back to his bedroom ready to tell Drew about someone else who had seen my ass this week when my phone rang. It was my agent. I grabbed my phone and answered it, still proceeding to the bedroom as I talked. "Hey Rick, what's up?" On the other end of the line, he was ecstatic. "Moll, I got it! I've got what you've been dreaming about! I've got you an audition at WLS, ABC-7." It was my favorite station in Chicago. "Oh my God! Rick, are you serious?" He started in on how I needed to get there next week. I had to tell Drew. "Hold on Rick, Drew, my agent got me an interview in Chicago next week! They're looking for a morning anchor and they love my tape." Drew was visually excited for me and I leaned over and hugged him with my phone. "Oh Rick, this is such great news, but I'm in the middle of something. Can I call you back tomorrow? I really want to learn more about the job. Thank you so much Rick."

Drew's excitement was gone now and he put some pants on and walked outside to smoke. I followed behind him because I didn't care who saw me half nude at this point. I was going to work in Chicago. "That's amazing Moll, it's your dream. I'm so proud of you. You deserve it, you've worked so hard." I could tell he wasn't buying what he was saying. "What's wrong? Oh Drew, please tell me what's wrong? I'm so excited right now, I think I want go back to bed and celebrate." I moved closer to him and rubbed his chest. "This is awesome news, let's get cleaned up and head to the airport. You've got a lot of preparing to do. If you don't get that gig, I'll kick your ass." And it wasn't until that moment that I got it. Chicago is just as far from Mobile as where I am now. What we just started was about to end. I stood outside and grabbed one his cigarettes. I lit it and started to pace. My dream job versus someone I really care about. He can give me everything I ever wanted except this. My dream job can fulfill everything I've ever aspired too.

I stepped into the shower with him and we just held each other. We both knew what this all meant, and we both knew what I was going to choose.

CHAPTER 23
GOOD-BYE

We didn't say anything in the car ride to the airport. We just held hands and looked out the windshield. It was more than somber, it was tragic. We parked and he carried my bags to the security point. Other than, "I'll get that" or "what a beautiful day," nothing was said. When we arrived at the roped off security canal, I realized he still had his glasses on. I couldn't tell if he was crying but the thought of him crying made me start crying. "I don't want to go; I want to stay with you. I've never felt this way before and I don't want this feeling to end." Drew took his glasses off and thankfully he wasn't crying. "Look, don't get upset we'll get together real soon. You've got a big task ahead of you; making sure that news director sees how amazing you are. You've been talking about Chicago since the first day I met you, and quite frankly, it's a cheaper flight."

He smiled and I fell into his chest. Why was he consoling me? Oh, he's the one that's had it rough. "When you interviewed in Boston and didn't take the job, did you regret it?" Drew looked away. "Let's not do this. Me, turning a job down is totally different than you going after your dream. Plus I don't care where you are, I'm just a flight away." I started crying again but this time I started to kiss him frantically. "I care about you so much, just hold me, please just hold me." He squeezed me as I soaked his shirt in tears.

After a long kiss good-bye, I put my bag on the conveyor belt and waved good-bye. I couldn't turn around and look at him, it would be too hard. I made it to my gate, and started to cry again. Why now I thought? Why is everything happening at the most awful time? I wanted to be with him, but I want that job. I boarded the plane and laid my head against the window and let my mind race. "Life is what happens to you while you're busy making other plans." It was a quote from John Lennon that Drew liked to recite. It was so true.

I finally arrived in Cedar Rapids and began to walk out the gate, to the lobby, and to the parking lot. All of a sudden, someone tapped me on the shoulder and asked for the time. The voice was familiar but I didn't look up. I was too distracted by everything. "Thanks Moll, can I get a ride too?" My head slowly raised and my mouth opened as I realized it was him. "I told you we'd see each other soon." I stopped him from talking, "Wait you said this was the last flight of the night. What are you doing here?" He shook his head," I said it was the last flight out of Mobile; I didn't say it was the last flight of the night. I flew out of Pensacola and beat you by an hour." I was stymied, I didn't know if I should hug, kiss, or hit him for stalking me. "But Drew, what are you doing? How can we make this work?"

He grinned again. "I moved with a woman to meet you. Now I'm thinking about moving to be with you. We need an office in Chicago anyway; it's a good place to be. They might have friendly faces in the morning. We held each other and kissed for so long. I heard a teenager say "go get a room." But we didn't care, because what we started was beginning all over again.

ABOUT THE AUTHOR

After spending more than a decade in TV news, this is J.W. Carter's first attempt at long-format fiction. J.W. was born in Thousand Oaks, California; raised in Marlboro, Massachusetts; attended high school in Mobile, Alabama; and graduated from the University of Memphis in Tennessee. The Carter family now calls Hudson, Iowa home.

10426337R0

Made in the USA
Lexington, KY
22 July 2011